THREE TO ONE ODDS

"I have killed a man," Laurie said. "Back east, before I came here."

"With a gun?" Clint asked.

"Yes."

Clint believed her. She was the one he had to worry about in this threesome.

"It's time for you to take off your gun belt," she said to him.

"Mmm, I don't think so."

"What?"

"I can't do that."

"Why not?"

"You'll kill me."

"We're going to kill you, anyway."

"That's my point," he said. "Why take off my gun if you're going to shoot me, anyway? I might as well take one or two of you with me."

"What?" Bette asked.

"Laurie," Cassie said, "make him take it off."

"I'm going to turn and draw my gun, ladies," he said, calmly. "Any of you who are pointing a gun at me when I do will die. It's as simple as that . . ."

DON'T MISS THESE
ALL-ACTION WESTERN SERIES
FROM THE BERKLEY PUBLISHING GROUP

THE GUNSMITH by J. R. Roberts
Clint Adams was a legend among lawmen, outlaws, and ladies.
They called him . . . the Gunsmith.

LONGARM by Tabor Evans
The popular long-running series about U.S. Deputy Marshal
Long—his life, his loves, his fight for justice.

SLOCUM by Jake Logan
Today's longest-running action Western. John Slocum rides
a deadly trail of hot blood and cold steel.

BUSHWHACKERS by B. J. Lanagan
An action-packed series by the creators of Longarm! The
rousing adventures of the most brutal gang of cutthroats ever
assembled—Quantrill's Raiders.

DIAMONDBACK by Guy Brewer
Dex Yancey is Diamondback, a southern gentleman turned
con man when his brother cheats him out of the family fortune. Ladies love him. Gamblers hate him. But nobody pulls
one over on Dex . . .

WILDGUN by Jack Hanson
Will Barlow's continuing search for his daughter, kidnapped
by the Blackfeet Indians who slaughtered the rest of his family.

THE GUNSMITH

226

WANTED: CLINT ADAMS

J. R. ROBERTS

JOVE BOOKS, NEW YORK

This is a work of fiction. Names, characters, places, and incidents are either the product of the author's imagination or are used fictitiously, and any resemblance to actual persons, living or dead, business establishments, events, or locales is entirely coincidental.

WANTED: CLINT ADAMS

A Jove Book / published by arrangement with
the author

PRINTING HISTORY
Jove edition / October 2000

The Penguin Putnam Inc. World Wide Web site address is
http://www.penguinputnam.com

ISBN: 0-515-12933-X

A JOVE BOOK®
Jove Books are published by The Berkley Publishing Group,
a division of Penguin Putnam Inc.,
375 Hudson Street, New York, New York 10014.
JOVE and the "J" design
are trademarks belonging to Penguin Putnam Inc.

PRINTED IN THE UNITED STATES OF AMERICA

10 9 8 7 6 5 4 3 2 1

ONE

Clint Adams had been shot at before—so many times he couldn't possibly keep count. Even as he was thinking this, his body was reacting instinctively, leaping from the saddle, tucking and rolling to minimize whatever injury he might incur from the fall. He was also hoping that none of the bullets would strike his new horse, Eclipse. He hadn't even really gotten the Darley Arabian completely broken in yet.

The horse was smart enough to run off, though, and get itself out of range of the shooting.

Clint scrambled along the ground until he found some kind of cover behind an outcropping of rocks, and drew his gun. He took a moment to take stock of his condition. Aside from some bumps that would turn into bruises, and some scrapes, he was fine. He'd known some men to break arms or legs falling from a horse, and more than enough of them who had broken their backs, or worse, their necks.

His assailant had not ceased fire when Clint hit the ground, but continued to shoot. Now that he had found cover, though, the shooting had stopped. Perhaps the gunman was even reloading. From the sound of the shots

1

Clint assumed that whoever was trying to kill him was using a rifle. That meant that he could have been anywhere, and could certainly have been out of range of his own handgun. He thought about his rifle, still in a scabbard on his saddle, much too far away to do him any good. He was going to have to try to locate the assailant and then get closer to him. That meant making himself a target again and then trying to pinpoint his attacker's location.

He looked around for another point of cover he could run to. He was going to have to run real fast, but judging from the man's shooting so far—and he assumed that the assailant was a man—he wasn't exactly a sharpshooter, or he would have taken him out of the saddle with one shot.

He spotted a stand of trees that would serve as good cover, took a deep breath and ran for them. The shooting started again and bullets started to strike the dirt behind him as the assailant tried to track him. He dove for the trees and made it. The shooting went on for several more seconds, and then stopped.

One man. That's what the maneuver had told him. Judging from the speed at which the bullets had come, they'd been fired by one man, firing as fast as he could with a rifle.

He had also pinpointed the man's location. He was firing from a hill about forty yards away. This further pointed out that the man was far from a crack shot. From that distance, with a rifle, a good shot would have only had to use one.

Now all he had to do was break cover and get around behind the poor marksman without being seen, because the closer he got to the man the more chance there was of finally catching a bullet.

He started looking for a route behind the man. He spotted a gulley that was deep enough to hide him. He didn't know where it would lead, but he could get to it while continuing to keep the trees between him and the shooter. Once in the gully he'd follow it and see where it lead.

Jeff Hardy was cursing his own stupidity. He'd fired too soon, warning the Gunsmith and giving him time to find cover. Hardy knew he wasn't a good shot, but he'd panicked. This was not something he ordinarily did, but the opportunity had been too good to pass up. He was twenty-three and everyone in the town of Limestone, Nebraska, had said he'd never amount to anything.

He saw this as a chance to prove all of them wrong— but he'd already messed it up. Maybe they weren't wrong about him. Maybe he *was* just a waste. Right now, though, he couldn't stop to think about that. The Gunsmith was somewhere behind that stand of trees. He just had to keep watching and wait for the man to show himself again and maybe this time he'd get in a lucky shot.

Maybe.

The gully was perfect. It even curved around so that when Clint reached the end of it he was alongside the hill and not in front of it. As he climbed out he was out of sight of the shooter, who he could now see laying on top of the hill. The man was sighting down the barrel of his rifle, waiting for Clint to show himself again. Even as Clint watched, the man wiped some sweat from his brow with a sleeve. It wasn't that warm, but the man was getting sweat in his eyes. He was nervous, and not good at this, so he had every right to be.

Clint moved around behind the hill and found the man's horse tied at the base of it to a small tree. He shushed the animal before it could make a sound and then started up the hill. He was hoping to reach the top before the man saw or heard him and get the drop on him. He wanted to find out why the man was shooting at him, and who—if anyone—had put him up to it.

He made his way quietly but for some reason—maybe the animal had picked up the scent of a predator in the area—the man's horse kicked up a fuss at the base of the hill. The shooter turned, saw Clint coming up the hill, and hurriedly brought his rifle around—but he was too slow.

"Don't do it!" was all Clint had time to say, and then he had no choice. As the man tried to get to his knees and bring his rifle to bear Clint fired and hit him in the chest. His arms flew up, his gun went flying, and he fell over backward and tumbled ass-over-tea kettle down the hill.

"Damn!" Clint shouted.

He ran to the top of the hill and looked down. The angle the man was lying at made it clear that, even if the bullet hadn't killed him, he was dead. Clint picked up the fallen rifle and went back down the hill to check out what he already knew. The man was dead.

He went back around the hill, recovered the man's horse—a worn and tired bay—and walked it around to the other side, where its owner lay. He slid the rifle back into its scabbard on the tired horse, then holstered his own gun, which he'd kept in his hand as a precaution, just in case the man had a partner somewhere.

Finally, he checked the man more thoroughly and found him to be little more than a boy, perhaps twenty-two or -three. He went through the dead man's pockets but came up with nothing, not even a two-bit piece.

Next he searched the man's saddlebags, and didn't come up with much, not even an extra shirt, until he felt a piece of paper at the bottom. He drew it out. It was folded in four and when he unfolded it he found himself looking at a wanted poster. He almost cast it aside, thinking it of no interest to him, when something made him stop to look at the front of it.

"What the hell—" he said.

The face on the poster was his. It was a drawing, but it was a very good one, plainly him, and if that wasn't evident enough his name was on the poster in black and white: CLINT ADAMS.

And at the bottom it said: WANTED DEAD OR ALIVE.

TWO

Clint rode into the nearest town, which was Limestone, with the young man tied to his saddle. He had the wanted poster folded up and tucked into his shirt pocket. He knew he was taking a chance by riding into town. These posters could have been all over the place but even if they were, it was all a mistake.

He wasn't wanted anywhere, that he knew of. There was no indication on the poster as to who had put it out. The reward was twenty-five hundred dollars. That was high. Whoever wanted him wanted him bad. Somebody had put up two thousand five hundred dollars for his head. But the poster gave no indication who it was. That was something he was going to have to find out, and soon, before someone else took it into their head to try and collect.

He rode down the main street with the body on the horse. That was not something you could do and not attract attention. People stopped and stared, and he hoped he'd encounter the sheriff's office before he had to stop and ask someone where it was.

He saw the undertaker's office, but he wasn't ready to stop there just yet. He'd make that his second choice, after

7

the sheriff's office, or if he couldn't find the sheriff, himself.

Finally, he spotted the local law's office and stopped both horses right in front of it. Men had begun to follow him to see where he was going to end up, and before he could dismount to enter the sheriff's office a man began to bang on the door and tell the sheriff he better get out here.

"What's goin' on?" a man asked, appearing in the doorway.

"Some fella's gone and killed young Jeff Hardy."

Well, that answered one question. The dead boy was certainly known in town.

Clint dismounted as the sheriff approached him. He was a big, competent-looking man in his late thirties.

"You got somethin' you wanna tell me?" he asked Clint.

"I do," Clint said, "but in your office, not out here."

"Why not?"

"I don't like crowds," Clint said, and then added, "especially hostile ones."

"Well," the sheriff said, "everybody here knew Jeff Hardy. He was a good boy."

"Is that so?" Clint asked. "Well, your good boy tried to ambush me, Sheriff."

"I find that hard to believe," the sheriff said. "Hell, I don't even know if Jeff knew how to shoot."

"Lucky for me," Clint said, "he didn't."

The sheriff sized him up, then turned and said, "Some of you boys get Jeff over to the undertaker. The rest of you go on about your business."

"Why'd he killed Jeff, Sheriff?" someone yelled out.

"That's what I'm aimin' to find out," the lawman said. "All right, Mister, let's go into the office."

• • •

Clint told his story without introducing himself. The sheriff sat and listened in silence until Clint was done.

"I gotta tell ya," the sheriff said, then, "I find this hard to believe of Jeff Hardy. Why would he try to ambush you?"

"Maybe this will explain it."

Clint took out the wanted poster and handed it to the sheriff. He watched while the man unfolded it, registered surprise that it was a wanted poster, and then even more surprise when he saw the name. He looked up at Clint a couple of times, and back down at the poster, and Clint knew that he was comparing his face to the drawing on the poster.

"You're Clint Adams?"

"That's right."

The lawman turned the poster over, looked at the back, and then at the front again.

"But I'm not wanted for anything, Sheriff," Clint said.

"That you know of, you mean," the lawman said.

"No, I mean I'm not wanted. I haven't done anything that would make me wanted," Clint explained.

"Not by the law, maybe."

"What?"

"Did you look close at this poster?"

"Well, I saw my picture and my name . . ."

"Look again, then," the lawman said, handing it back.

Clint took a long, close looked at the poster and saw what the sheriff was getting at.

"It's phony," he said.

"That's right," the sheriff said. "So while you may not be wanted by the law, somebody has gone through all the trouble of making it look like you are."

"What the hell—" Clint said.

"Obviously," the sheriff said, "somebody wants you dead bad enough to pay twenty-five hundred dollars."

THREE

"I don't know why I didn't notice right away," Clint said. "The paper is different than most posters, and it doesn't say who to contact for the reward."

"A lot of people wouldn't notice that," the sheriff said. "They'd seen the amount and it's only after that they'd start wondering where to go to collect. Somebody is counting on people's greed."

Clint sat down heavily across from the sheriff.

"I'm used to being shot at for a reason I can understand," Clint said, "but this . . . I have no idea who'd do this, or why."

"Well, it looks like you're gonna have find out, or there are a lot more Jeff Hardys in your future."

"You're right about that."

The sheriff handed Clint back the phony wanted poster.

"I'll accept your story about what happened with young Jeff," he said. "He's been complaining about not having enough money to ask his girl to marry him. He would have seen this as a way to get some quick cash, and he's the perfect dupe for this. He wouldn't have worried about where to get the money until after he'd done the deed."

"He was looking to get married, huh?"

11

"I'm afraid so."

Clint stood up.

"I suppose I should go and see his girl."

"I don't know that that would be such a good idea."

"I need to tell her I didn't mean to kill him," Clint said. "He gave me no choice. Also, maybe she can tell me where he got the poster."

The sheriff stood up and reached for his hat.

"What are you doing?"

"I better go with you," the lawman said. "I don't think she'd see you, otherwise."

"I appreciate that, Sheriff."

"I'm doing it for her, Adams," he said.

"I don't care why you're doing it," Clint said, "just that you are. By the way, what's you name?"

"Dave Starr," the lawman said. "Sheriff Starr."

"Well, I won't be in your town long, Sheriff," Clint promised. "Just long enough to see if anyone knows where this poster came from."

They went outside and the sheriff pointed to his right.

"There's somethin' else you might think about," he said, as they walked along.

"What's that?"

"You seem to be genuinely upset about killin' young Hardy."

"I am."

"Well, maybe that's what somebody wants."

"You mean," Clint said, "they're setting me up to have to kill some innocent men like him?"

"Takes all kinds to try and collect a bounty," the sheriff said. "Bounty hunters, sure, but also desperate people, like Jeff. And who knows? One of them might even get lucky."

"Now that thought," Clint admitted, "had crossed my mind."

∙ ∙ ∙

They went to the girl's home but she wasn't there. Apparently, someone had already brought her the news, and she had gone to the undertaker's with her mother and father.

When Clint and the sheriff arrived at the undertaker's office there was a crowd of people there.

"This might not be such a good idea," Sheriff Starr said.

"And maybe it is," Clint said. "I'll explain the situation to them and show them the poster. You can back me up that the poster is a phony. Maybe someone will know where the boy got it."

Starr thought a moment, then said, "All right. That may work."

They entered the undertaker's office, the sheriff first and then Clint. There must have been people there who had seen Clint ride into town because someone shouted out, "There's the man what killed Jeff!"

The crowd of people in the place turned to look at Clint.

"Let's string him up!" someone yelled.

"Now, hold on," Sheriff Starr shouted, raising his hands. "Before you string anybody up you gotta listen to his story."

"Do we?"

A man stepped forward. Gray-haired, in his fifties, face wracked with pain, this had to be Jeff Hardy's father. Behind him an older woman stood with her arms around a younger one. Mother and girlfriend, no doubt.

"Did you kill my son?" the man demanded of Clint.

"Yes, I did."

"Then why do I have to listen to your story?"

"Because," Clint said, "he gave me no choice. He tried to bushwack me with a rifle."

"Liar!" the young girl shouted. "Jeff couldn't shoot."

"I know that, Miss . . . now. I'm truly sorry for your loss, all of you, but it happened as I say it did. He tried to shoot me, gave me no choice but to defend myself. I'm sorry."

"Why?" the older man asked. "Why would my son try to shoot you?"

"Because of this."

Clint took out the poster and handed it to the man, who took it, stared at it, then looked at the sheriff.

"Not only did he kill my son, but he's a wanted man?"

"The poster is a phony, Aaron," Starr said to the man. "Look at the amount on it, man. Wouldn't that have solved all Jeff's problems? Wouldn't that have been enough to get married on?"

Aaron Hardy turned to look at his wife and his once future daughter-in-law. The young girl, thinking he was staring at her, broke down.

"Yes, yes, yes!" she shouted. "All right, yes. I knew Jeff had the poster, and that he was going to try to collect the reward."

"He couldn't track," the sheriff said, "and he couldn't shoot. It was just dumb luck that he crossed paths with Mr. Adams."

Hardy's mother wasn't listening. She pushed the younger girl away and stared at her with distaste.

"Jeff wouldn't have gotten an idea like that on his own," she said, accusingly. "You did it. You put my son up to this, didn't you. Didn't you?"

The girl couldn't answer. She fell to her knees, wracked with sobs, muttering what might have been "I'm sorry" over and over again from behind her hands.

"You're dead to me now," Hardy's mother said, coldly. "Just as dead as my son is."

She marched from the undertaker's office and her husband, who paused only to return the poster to Clint, followed. The girl remained on her knees as the rest of the people filed out. No one called for Clint to be strung up anymore.

Soon, only Clint, the sheriff, the undertaker and the girl were left. In a back room Jeff Hardy was stretched out on a table. It was quiet except for the girl's sobs.

FOUR

"Janie," the sheriff said.

The girl continued to sob.

"Janie," Starr said again, "come on. Get up."

The girl turned a tearstained face up to them and said, "I didn't want him to get killed. We just needed the money."

"I know, girl," Starr said, "but we need to know something."

She sniffed and asked, "What?"

"Where did he get the poster?" Clint asked. "Who gave it to him?"

"It was Bo," she said, sniffing.

"Bo Shannon?" Starr asked.

She nodded.

Starr looked at Clint and said, "Jeff's best friend."

"Where is he?" Clint asked.

"Well," Starr said, "he *was* here, a minute ago. He left with the others."

"He probably knows we're going to be looking for whoever gave Jeff that poster," Clint said. "Maybe he's going to leave town for a while . . . at least, until I leave."

"The livery," Starr said.

17

"You get her up and send her home," Clint said. "I'll check the livery."

"You don't know what he looks like."

"I'll look for a boy Jeff's age, saddling his horse in a real hurry."

Clint found his way to the livery stable on foot. Sure enough, as he entered, a young man was hurriedly saddling a horse who wouldn't stand still.

"Come on, you damn bag o' bones," he swore at the horse. "Stand still."

"Going somewhere?" Clint asked.

The boy turned, saw Clint and froze. His eyes flicked all around the livery, but his legs wouldn't move.

"Don't kill me!" he pleaded.

Clint came closer to the boy, whose back was up against the horse, which had finally decided to stand still.

"I'm not going to kill you," Clint said.

"You killed Jeff."

"Because he shot at me. Why would I kill you?"

"I-I-I don't know."

"Did you shoot at me too?"

"N-no!"

"Did you put him up to it?"

He looked away and said, "No."

"Oh," Clint said, "I get it now. He got the poster from you, didn't he?"

The boy didn't answer.

"Didn't he!" Clint shouted.

"Yes!"

"Good," Clint said. "Now all you have to do is tell me where you got it from."

"Wha-what?"

"I want to know where you got it."

"Y-you're not gonna kill me?"

"Not if you tell me what I want to know."

"Okay, I got it—"

"Unless, of course, you lie to me."

The boy hesitated, then said, "H-how will you know?"

"Because," Clint said, touching the boy's sweaty cheek, "if you lie to me you'll sweat, and you won't be able to look me in the eye."

"I-I'm sweatin' 'cause I'm nervous," the boy said. "I-I'm scared."

Clint grabbed the boy's ear and twisted it.

"Ow!"

"Don't lie to me, Bo," he said. "Understand?"

"Yes, yes, I understand . . . ow!"

Clint released his ear.

"Go ahead," he said, "tell me where you got the poster."

FIVE

"Do you believe him?" Sheriff Starr asked Clint.

"Yes."

"Why?"

"Because he was scared," Clint said. "The boy didn't exactly strike me as the brave type."

"He's not," Starr said. "Okay, so some fella was passin' through town and handed out the posters in the saloon. That means that lots of the men in town got them."

"Most men aren't affected by reward postings," Clint said. "You've got to have it in you to go after a reward."

"Or you've got to be desperate for money," the sheriff said, "like Jeff was."

"Or have a woman pushing you."

"Usually," Starr said, "havin' a woman push you isn't a bad thing."

"Are you married?"

"Yes."

"Well," Clint said, "I guess it depends on what she's pushing you to do."

"So what are you gonna do now?"

"I've got to track this fellow with the posters."

"How?"

21

"By following the posters," Clint said. "You have a telegraph office, so I'll start that way. In fact, maybe you can help."

"If I can."

"You can send some telegrams up and down the line to the lawmen in other towns nearby, see if any of these posters have shown up."

"I can do that."

"You can also let them know that the posters are phonies."

"All right. What will you be doing in the meantime?"

"I'll stay overnight," he said, "and see if you get any answers by morning. If you have, then maybe I'll know what direction to go in."

"If you're gonna stay the night," Starr said, "you better remember that there are other copies of that poster floating around town, and by now everyone knows that you're here."

"I'm aware of that," Clint said. "I'll have to take that chance. Do you know anyone else in town brave enough—or dumb enough—to come after me? Anybody else getting married soon who needs money?"

"Not that I know of," Starr said, "but if I think of somethin' I'll let you know."

"Thanks," Clint said. "How many hotels do you have in town?"

"One."

"Then you know where I'll be," Clint said.

"Yeah," Sheriff Starr said, "and so does everyone else."

SIX

"You're such a coward," Janie Hansen told Bo Shannon.

He shuffled his feet and said, "Come on, Janie. He's the Gunsmith."

"I don't care who he is," she said. "He's a man, and he can be killed by a bullet."

"I s'pose."

"It's a lucky break for us, Bo, that he's in town."

"Wasn't so lucky for Jeff."

"Jeff was a boy," Janie said. She went to Bo, took his face in her hands and kissed him. She let her tongue slide into his mouth and pressed her crotch to his. "You're a man."

He tried to put his arms around her but she slipped away.

"Oh, no," she said. "No more until the Gunsmith is dead and we have that money. Do you know what we can do with two thousand five hundred dollars, Bo?"

"What?"

"We could leave Limestone forever," she said. "You want to leave, don't you?"

"I don't know . . ."

"Well, you want me, don't you?"

He looked at her hungrily. Janie was the prettiest girl he'd ever seen, but she was Jeff's girl. Or she *was* Jeff's girl.

"I sure do," he said. He'd always been jealous of Jeff that he had Janie.

"And I want to leave," she said. "You'll take me away from here once we have the money, won't you, Bo?"

"I sure will, Janie."

They were in a clearing just outside of town, so that no one would see them talking together. Janie was supposed to be distraught over Jeff's death, and upset at the way his mother had spoken to her. In truth, Janie Hansen was a good little actress, used to getting her way with the boys. She used to do it all the time when she was younger, and when she got older it got even easier to control them because she used sex.

"We'll go to San Francisco, or New York."

"Or Tombstone!" Bo said, excitedly.

"No," she said, shaking her head, "Tombstone is nothing. We want to go to the big cities, like Chicago, and New Orleans. Maybe even to Europe."

"Europe?" he said. "Where's that?"

"Across the ocean," she said. "Never mind. We're not going anywhere until Clint Adams is dead."

"I can't believe that Jeff just ran into him," Bo said.

"He didn't."

"What?"

"He didn't just run into him," she said. "The man who gave him the poster told him that Adams was headed this way."

"Jeff never told me that."

"That's because he didn't want to share the money with you," Janie said.

"But . . . we was best friends."

"I guess you weren't as close as you thought."

In fact, it was Janie who'd convinced Jeff not to say

anything to his best friend, Bo, about the Gunsmith heading this way. It was she who didn't want to share the money with anyone. In fact, she didn't want to share it with Jeff, either. Once they had it, and they had left Limestone, she was going to find a way to grab the money and leave him stranded somewhere along the way.

Now she'd do that to Bo.

But first . . .

She moved close to Bo again, and this time she let him touch her. He held her tight, smelled her hair, felt the heat from her body right through their clothes.

"I want to share it with you, though," she said. "And I want to share something else with you, too, Bo."

"What?"

She slid her hands between them and unfastened his pants. In a second she had his trousers down around his ankles, and his swollen penis in her hand. With her other hand she fondled his heavy testicles. This might not be so bad, after all. Jeff had been the better-looking one, but now she knew that Bo was the better built.

"This," she said, and opened her mouth to take him inside.

"Jesus," Bo said, getting up on his toes while she sucked on him, and slid her hands down along his thighs, up the back to dig her nails into his buttocks.

She knew Bo Shannon would do anything she wanted, now.

SEVEN

Clint took Eclipse to the livery and made sure he was well taken care of before walking to the hotel and getting himself a room. Once he was in his room, looking out the window, he realized how hungry he was. He hoped he was going to be able to get a decent meal in town. True, he'd managed to convince Jeff Hardy's parents that he'd had no choice but to kill their son, but he didn't know how the rest of the town was going to feel about it.

He went downstairs to take a look at the hotel dining room, decided that it looked clean and decent enough and went in. There were other diners there, but they were guests in the hotel like he was, not residents of the town. For this reason they didn't know that he had killed Jeff Hardy, and they paid more attention to their dinners than to him.

The scathing look he got from the waiter who took his order, though, was enough to tell him that there were still people in town who didn't look upon him kindly after what he'd done, no matter what the reason might have been.

The dinner was edible, the coffee drinkable. That was

the best he could say about the meal. Still, it satisfied his hunger pains, and that was what mattered.

When he left the dining room he wasn't sure whether he wanted to brave going to the saloon for a drink, or if he should just go to his room. It was early, though, so he wouldn't be able to sleep, and he would be bored in his room. He decided to go ahead and try the saloon, see what kind of a reception he got.

On the way to the saloon, though, he passed the telegraph office and decided to go in and send some telegrams of his own.

Across the street from the hotel, Bo Shannon was hiding in a doorway. He watched as Clint Adams left and started walking up the street. He would have stayed in that doorway and hidden forever, but he could still smell Janie's hair, taste her mouth, and *feel* her mouth on him. Because of all that he left the doorway and followed Clint, watched him go into the telegraph office. Bo had help coming, three friends of his to whom he had promised a piece of the reward.

He'd reminded Janie of what the sheriff had told Jeff's parents, about the poster being a phony.

"That was a lie," she told him, urgently. "The sheriff probably wants the money for himself, but we're gonna get it, Bo! You and me, we're gonna get it and spend it all together."

"After we give the boys their share," Bo reminded her.

"Oh, of course," she said, "that's right, after your friends get their share."

He crossed the street to take up a position in a doorway across from the telegraph office. All he had to do was keep an eye on Adams until the boys got there. When there were four of them, then they could decide the best way to take him.

He was scared, because this was the Gunsmith, but

when he closed his eyes, thought about him and Janie together, he got brave again . . . for a little while.

Clint sent several telegrams, one of which went to his friend Rick Hartman in Labyrinth, Texas. If anyone could track down the origin of those posters it would be Rick. He also sent one to Denver, to his friend Talbot Roper. Roper was the best private detective in the business, although no one would ever convince old Allan Pinkerton of that. Telegrams went out also to other friends who might be able to help, including Bat Masterson and Luke Short. Maybe somebody had seen a poster, or heard about it, and knew something helpful. Of course, he had no way of knowing how far and how wide these posters had been spread. The telegrams would also help him determine that.

Bo Shannon's description of the man who had given Jeff Hardy the poster wasn't very helpful. He'd said the man was of medium height and weight, and sort of "normal" looking, with no distinguishing marks or features. That description could have fit dozens—hundreds—of men.

Once the telegrams were sent he left the telegraph office and started for the saloon again. He craved a cold beer, and maybe at the saloon he'd be able to find somebody else who had been given a poster, someone who'd be better equipped to give him a good description of the man who was passing them out.

EIGHT

When Clint entered the saloon—like the hotel, the only one in Limestone—he knew he was immediately the center of attention. There was some buzzing of conversation as those who knew told those who didn't know that this was the man who had killed Jeff Hardy.

He walked to the bar and ordered a beer. The bartender hesitated, but when he got a hard look from Clint he drew the beer and put it on the bar. He slapped it down hard, so that some of the beer slopped over. Hoping that he had saved face by doing so he moved to another part of the bar.

". . . got some nerve comin' in here," Clint heard a man mutter.

He turned and, very matter of factly, asked, "Who said that?"

No answer. There were fifteen or twenty men in the place, and they all found something else to look at.

"Come on, now," Clint said. "You've all been staring at me. Somebody was brave enough to say it behind my back. Isn't anyone brave enough to say it to my face?"

Apparently not.

Clint did notice one man looking at him, though, while

the others looked away. He was sitting at a table with two other men, one beefy hand wrapped around a beer mug. He had a heavy black beard and sunken eyes, and was dressed like a farmer. As Clint approached he saw that the man had no gun.

"What about you, friend?" Clint asked. "You look brave. Was it you?"

The man looked up and locked eyes with Clint, then stood up, towering over him. He must have stood six and a half feet tall, with biceps like cannonballs. Clint thought he might have found the town blacksmith.

"Yeah, it was me," the man said. "You got some nerve comin' in here after what you done."

"And just what did I do?"

"You know what you done," the man said. "You killed young Jeff Hardy."

"Only because he left me no choice," Clint said.

"That's what you say."

Clint put his beer down on the table and took the poster from his pocket. He unfolded it and held it out so everyone could see it.

"He took some shots at me, and after I defended myself I found this in his saddlebags. Anybody else have one of these?"

No answer.

"Maybe somebody else wants to try to collect?"

His question was met by silence.

"How about you?" he asked the big, bearded man. "You want to collect on this bounty?"

"I ain't no bounty hunter," the man said, "and I ain't got a gun."

"I can see you don't have a gun," Clint said, "but even if you did, you couldn't collect on this bounty. Know why?"

"Because you're so danged fast with your gun?"

"No," Clint said. "Because there is no bounty."

"What are you talkin' about?" the man asked.

"This poster is a fake," Clint said, "made up by some-body who's got it in for me. Somebody was here in town, passing these things out, and he gave Jeff Hardy one." Clint folded it and put it back in his pocket. "That's what got Jeff Hardy killed, a bounty that doesn't exist."

That started some conversation up among the men.

"Now, what I want to do is find the man who was passing these out," Clint said. "Then through him I want to find whoever did put the poster out, because in the end that's who killed Jeff Hardy."

The men continued to talk amongst themselves in low tones. The bearded man continued to stand in front of Clint.

"I need somebody to describe the man to me," Clint said. "I can't find him if I don't know what he looks like."

He waited. When no one spoke immediately, he went on.

"I also need to talk to anyone who talked with him," Clint said. "Maybe you have some idea of which way he's headed."

Still no reply. He picked up his beer.

"I'm going to go back to the bar and finish my beer," Clint said. "Anyone who has anything to say can join me, and I'll buy you one."

He locked eyes with the big, bearded man again, then turned and walked to the bar.

NINE

Clint stood at the bar for an hour before someone joined him there. Unfortunately, it was Sheriff Dave Starr who walked in, spotted him and walked over.

"Buy you a beer, Sheriff?" Clint asked.

"Sure, why not?"

The bartender brought the sheriff one, and Clint a fresh one.

"Took a pretty big chance comin' in here," Starr said.

"I don't think so."

"Folks hereabouts thought pretty highly of Jeff Hardy."

"Nobody in here is ready to do anything but stare and mumble," Clint said. "I think I'm pretty safe."

Starr looked around the place and said, "Yeah, you might be right, at that. If his own father didn't go after you I guess this bunch won't." He turned back to the bar. "Still, you *will* be leavin' town tomorrow, won't you?"

Clint looked at him.

"Are you telling me to leave town tomorrow?"

"Nope," Starr said, "I guess I'm just thinkin' out loud."

"I sent some telegrams, Sheriff," Clint said. "I suppose if I don't hear anything by tomorrow I can leave town."

"I just think the longer you stay here, the braver somebody might get—and not everyone is gonna believe that poster is a fake."

"You're probably right."

"Speaking of telegrams, I did what you asked," Starr said. "I got answers from the sheriffs in the two towns nearest here to the south. Seems they had some posters show up there, too."

"When?"

"Apparently before they got here."

"So he's not travelling south, then," Clint said. "Guess I'll head north until I find evidence that he didn't go that way, either."

The sheriff put his mug down while it was still half full.

"I got rounds to make," he said. "Stop in and see me before you leave tomorrow. Maybe I'll have some more news for you."

"Okay, thanks."

Before he left Starr said, "And do me another favor. Don't stay here much longer, either. Whiskey has a way of making men brave."

"I know," Clint said. "I'll be turning in, soon."

" 'Nite, then."

Starr left and Clint took a look at the room in the mirror behind the bar. Some of the men were looking at him, but for the most part the room seemed to have forgotten about him.

"Not gonna get no takers tonight," the bartender said.

"Doesn't look like it."

"If you'd leave now," the man said, "I could stop holdin' my breath and gettin' ready to hit the floor."

Clint stared at the man a moment and then said, "Okay . . . but just for you."

He turned and went out the bat-wing doors, headed for his hotel.

•   •   •

Bo Shannon and three of his friends were waiting out in the darkness for Clint to leave the saloon. They saw the sheriff go in and one of them got skittish.

"He ain't gonna arrest him, is he?" Harve Barlow asked. "If he arrests him we lose our reward."

"He ain't gonna arrest him," Shannon said. "If he was gonna do that he'd've done it already. Just relax."

But Barlow and the others didn't relax until the sheriff came out alone and walked away.

"Okay," Barlow said, "now we go in?"

"No," Shannon said, "we're just gonna wait out here for him. I'd rather take him in the dark."

"Suits me," Sam Court said. "If I got to face the Gunsmith I'd rather do it in the dark when he don't know I'm comin'."

The others all agreed. They were getting skittish again when Clint finally came out.

"Okay," Shannon said, "let's do it."

The first shot was premature, and warned Clint they were coming. It didn't matter who fired it, because suddenly the night was lit up by muzzle flashes. Clint dropped to the ground and rolled behind a horse trough, waiting for the hail of bullets to stop. When they did he got to his knees and fired a few shots into the dark, where the bullets had come from. He knew he'd gotten lucky at least once when somebody cried out in pain.

He hadn't seen anyone leave the saloon in the hour since he'd made his offer of a drink for information, so whoever was shooting at him had probably been waiting outside a while. He was lucky that somebody had gotten nervous and fired too soon, or they might have taken him down with the hail of bullets that followed that first shot.

He dropped down behind the trough again, ejected the spent shells from his gun and fed in a live one. The sheriff was off making his rounds, and unless he was in on this he'd be showing up soon. If there were enough shooters, and they tried rushing him, Clint felt they would have a chance of taking him before the law arrived. It all depended on how smart the person leading them was.

Clint felt he couldn't afford even the few moments it would take to find out, though. He was going to have to make the first move.

TEN

They might have expected him to do a few things. He could hide, as he was doing, or try to run, or even try to get back into the saloon. Even now men were standing at the saloon doors and windows, trying to see what was happening. He doubted any of them would come out and try to offer him any assistance.

But the one thing they probably wouldn't expect him to do was rush *them*. Run right into a hail of bullets. That would unnerve them and give him an edge—provided he lived through it.

Even with his gun fully loaded, without covering fire he wouldn't be able to risk more than three shots while he was rushing. That would leave him three. If there were more than three shooters, he was going to be in trouble, but he had to take the chance.

He scooted over to the other side of the horse trough, counted to three, then stood up and charged, firing as he ran.

"Let's rush 'im!" Barlow said. He was gritting his teeth because one of Clint's shots had scraped his left arm. It wasn't a bad wound, but it hurt.

"He's got cover, and we don't," Shannon said. "Who fired that first shot, damn it?"

No one admitted to it.

"We're still in the dark," Sam Court said. "I say we wait him out."

"The sheriff probably heard the shots," the fourth man, Ed Woodley said, "He's gonna be here soon."

"Ed's right," Shannon said. "We've got to take him now. If we rush him we're bound to get him."

"And he's bound to get one or two of us," Court said. "I don't like the odds."

"Then come up with a better—" Bo Shannon was saying when Clint Adams stood up and charged them, firing his gun.

"What the hell—" Sam Court said, and started firing wildly.

Clint knew their initial shots were going wild. He also became aware of shots being fired from behind him by someone. At him? Or to cover him? He didn't know. All he knew was that none of them seemed to be coming close to him.

He kept running, fired his third and final shot. As he got closer he could see their shapes in the dark as they moved around. That was all he needed. Now he had targets. The bad thing was, he counted four!

"Aim, damn it!" Bo Shannon shouted. "You're not aimin'!"

"He's crazy—" Sam Barlow started, but a bullet struck him in the throat and his words drowned in his own blood.

"He got Sam!" Woodley screamed, and Shannon could hear the fear. He'd been trying to quell his own rising fear, but hearing it on the tone of one of the others opened the floodgates. Not only was Adams coming for them, but somebody else was firing at them, as well.

He turned and ran.

• • •

Clint fired a second shot into a silhouette and saw it spin and fall. A third became clearer as it ran into the light and away. He could fire at it, or the remaining one in front of the store ahead of him.

A fleeing man is no danger so, as a bullet tugged at his sleeve, he fired his final shot. He hit his target dead center, driving the man back and through the window of the store.

It grew quiet. Clint moved carefully forward, because his gun was empty.

"I got your back, Adams," a man said, from behind him.

He knew the voice. It was the deep, rumbling base of the big man he'd spoken to in the saloon.

When they reached the boardwalk he checked the two men on the ground, determined that they were dead. Then he climbed through the window of what turned out to be a hardware store and checked the third man, who was also dead. Only then did he look at the big man from the saloon.

"Much obliged for your help," he said, as the man holstered his gun.

"I just gave you some covering fire," the man said. "Couldn't just stand by and watch them gun you down."

"Thanks again," Clint said.

"One of them got away."

"I know," Clint said. "I didn't see who it was."

"What the hell—" Sheriff Dave Starr shouted, as he ran over to them. He stopped, out of breath. "I was all the way at the other end of town when I heard the shots. What the hell happened?"

"Four men tried to bushwack Adams on the street," the big man said.

Starr looked around and saw three bodies.

"Damn it!" he swore. "Where's the fourth?"

"Got away," Clint said. "I didn't see who it was, probably wouldn't have recognized him, anyway."

"I did," the big man said.

"You saw who it was?" Starr asked.

The man nodded.

"It was young Jeff Hardy's friend," he said, "that fella Shannon."

ELEVEN

In the morning Clint walked over to the sheriff's office.

"Did you identify the dead men?" Clint asked.

"Yeah," Starr said. "Their names won't mean anything to you, but they're pretty well known in the county."

"For hire?"

"Yeah, but not usually for bushwacking. Usually just some tough stuff. Bo must have offered them part of the reward."

"And what about Bo?" Clint asked.

"He's nowhere to be found."

"And Janie?"

"What about her?"

"Come on, Sheriff," Clint said. "You know she put him up to this, just like she pushed Hardy into going after me."

"I can't arrest her for that."

"But she could probably tell you where Bo is."

"Maybe," the lawman said. "I'll ask her."

"I could do that."

"No!" Starr blurted. "That's my job. I'll do it."

"Well," Clint said, "I'm going to hang around for a couple of more hours to see if I get any responses from my telegrams. After that I'll be going."

43

"Good," the sheriff said. "It's not that I blame you for what happened last night, but—"

"I understand, Sheriff," Clint said. "It wouldn't have happened if I wasn't here."

"That's true."

"Don't worry," Clint said, on his way to the door. "I'll be leaving before noon."

He opened the door, then stopped and said, "By the way."

"Yeah?"

"That fella that helped me last night. The big, bearded one."

"That was Henry Tate."

"He didn't have a gun when I saw him in the saloon," Clint said, "but he had a gun and holster on the street."

"He grabbed it from a man standing next to him," Starr said. "Borrowed it, I guess you might say."

"Where can I find him?" Clint asked. "He left before I could really say thanks to him."

"He runs the feed and grain store," Starr said. "Should be open by now."

"Thanks," Clint said. "I'll stop over there."

"Let me know when you're leaving," Starr said.

"You'll be the first, Sheriff."

As Clint entered the feed and grain store he saw Henry Tate with a huge burlap sack up on each shoulder.

"Be right with you," the big man said, without looking to see who his customer was.

Clint watched as the man hoisted the two sacks up onto a shelf as if they weighed nothing. When he was done he slapped his hands together to clean them and turned to see who his customer was.

"Oh, it's you," he said. "Don't guess you're here for feed or grain."

"I'm just here to say thanks properly."

"No need," Tate said. "I just couldn't watch a man get gunned down on the street. Four to one odds were too much for me to watch, even if everyone else could."

"Whatever your reason," Clint said, "I'd like to shake you hand and say thank you."

"Sure."

Tate came forward and swallowed Clint's hand up in one of his.

"I don't think I hit nothin'," Tate said, releasing Clint's hand. His grip had been firm, but controlled. He was not one to flaunt his great strength, apparently. "I ain't worth shit with a handgun."

"Just the fact that someone else was shooting at them caused them to hurry their shots," Clint said. "It really helped me out."

"Glad to help," Tate said. "Guess I was kind of hard on you in the saloon last night."

"That's okay," Clint said. "I understand how well-liked Jeff Hardy was."

"Hardy was a little shit, most of the time," Tate said. "It's funny how much better people get when they're dead."

"That's the way it usually happens," Clint said. "I guess it's better that the good gets remembered over the bad."

"I suppose. You gonna be leavin' town soon?"

"In a couple of hours," Clint said. "I don't want anyone else getting brave and shooting up the town trying to get to me."

"The sheriff find Shannon?"

"No, not yet."

"He's another one," Tate said.

"Another little shit?"

"Yeah," Tate said. "Both of them was just led around by the nose by that Janie. Now she's—"

"A little shit."

"A little tease," Tate said. "Maybe even more. I can't

imagine them boys doin' the things they done without gettin' at least a little taste."

"More than a taste, I'd think," Clint said, "to make them come after me like that."

"I guess you're right. Well, I got to get to work."

"I won't keep you," Clint said. "Just wanted to say my thanks proper."

"Good luck huntin' down whoever put out that paper on you."

"They're the ones who are going to need the luck when I find them," Clint said.

"Somehow," Tate said, "I don't doubt that you will."

TWELVE

Twenty minutes to noon Clint received a telegram from Rick Hartman. He was standing right outside the telegraph office when it came, so the clerk came out and handed it to him. It really wasn't worth waiting for. It said: CHECK-ING INTO ORIGIN OF POSTER. KEEP IN TOUCH. It was signed: RICK.

Nothing came from Masterson or anyone else by noon so, true to his word, he saddled up Eclipse and rode over to the sheriff's office.

"Ready to leave?" the sheriff asked as Clint entered.

"I'm on my way out of town now."

"Any word?"

"No," Clint said. "I'll send more telegrams along the way. Thanks for your help, Sheriff."

The two men shook hands.

"I'm afraid I didn't do much to help."

"You didn't lock me up for killing Jeff Hardy," Clint said. "That alone was a big help."

"Well, good luck," Starr said. "I hope you find the bastard who put that poster out."

"Don't worry," Clint said, "I'll find him. One way or another, I'll find him."

47

Clint left the office and mounted Eclipse. As he started out of town he saw a figure down the street that looked familiar. He rode back to talk to her.

"Janie," he said.

"What do you want?" she demanded, sullenly.

"Both your boys are gone, huh?" Clint asked. "Jeff's dead, and Bo is on the run. You should know that the poster on me is a phony."

"You say."

"If you send any more of your boyfriends after me you'll be getting them killed for nothing," he said. "There is no reward."

She folded her arms and glared up at him. She didn't look very pretty at that moment.

"I needed that money to get me out of this town," she said. She moved closer to the horse, then, and put her hand on his leg. Suddenly, her entire expression changed.

"Unless," she said, rubbing his thigh, "you take me with you?"

"I'm afraid I can't do that."

"Why not?" she asked. Her hand was warm through his pants. Looking down at her now he could see how she got young men to do what she wanted. Her eyes were shining, her lips were moist. When Janie turned on the seduction she was very formidable . . . if you were twenty-one.

He took her hand and lifted it off of him.

"I'm only interested in women, Janie," he said, "not girls."

He turned his horse and rode up the straight.

"Somebody will kill you!" she shouted after him. "You'll see."

He ignored her and rode out of town.

THIRTEEN

Three weeks after the incidents in Limestone, Nebraska, Clint stopped in a town called Graceful, Wyoming

Clint had followed the trail north for ten days before it suddenly swerved to the east and he found himself in Wyoming. Once there the trail turned to the south. Along the way he figured out that he was a few weeks behind the man with the posters—or men. He'd gotten different descriptions in different places, and had come to believe that although he was following the trail of posters, he was not following a single man.

This had been the hardest he'd pushed Eclipse since receiving the horse as a gift from P. T. Barnum in New York the year before, and the animal had responded well. However, the time had come to give him a rest.

Once he had Eclipse safely in the livery he went to the nearest hotel and got himself a room. He needed a bath, a drink, food, some rest, some time with the local sheriff and a telegraph office. Graceful—slightly larger than Limestone had been—offered all these things.

The talk with the sheriff had to come first, no matter how dirty, thirsty, hungry or tired he felt, just in case the posters had circulated well in this town. He left the hotel,

49

alert to his surroundings. It was bad enough that when people recognized him they sometimes took it as a challenge, but now there was a piece of paper floating around with $2500 on his head. The added incentive would be all some of them would need to get brave—and foolish, or worse . . . lucky.

When he reached the sheriff's office he found the door locked and no one answered when he knocked. He was able to look in the window, and it was obvious that the office was not deserted. He could see smoke rising from a pot-bellied stove. The man must have been out making rounds. He'd have to put this talk off until later.

Now that he was out he decided that a meal and a drink took precedence over a bath. He had passed a small cafe on the way to the sheriff's office, so he retraced his steps and went in. It was between meal times so getting seated and served was no problem. In no time he was eating a meal that, if nothing else, was hot. He took his time over it not because it was good, but because it was good to relax. When he was done he would stop into the telegraph office before going back to his hotel and finally having a bath.

He made it all the way back to the hotel without incident—a situation that was destined not to last.

Clint never took a bath without keeping his gun close by. This time, while he soaked, he hung his holster on the back of a chair, with the gun butt hanging toward him. This little fact saved his life. As the door to the bath room crashed open his hand immediately went for the gun. He drew it cleanly from the holster, wet hand closing tightly over the butt.

Quickly, he determined that none of the three men who had invaded his bath was wearing a badge. It was very important to him that he did not shoot a lawman. Since none of them was wearing a tin star, and all were holding guns, they were all fair game.

He fired first and a man went down. One of the others fired and the bullet made a hole in the tub. Only the water kept it from gouging a hole in Clint's leg. In point of fact the bullet did strike him, but because of the water it did not break the skin. It "bounced" off him.

He threw himself and the tub over and as the water flooded the room he fired from behind the overturned tub, striking both men in the chest. Both discharged their weapons as they died, one into the ceiling and the other into the floor.

Clint was standing over the bodies, naked, checking to make sure they were dead, when the desk clerk entered the room and surveyed the carnage, wide-eyed.

"Get the sheriff over here," Clint said. "Move!"

The clerk fled the room. Clint, dripping wet, naked and holding a gun, scared him silly and he was only too happy to go looking for the sheriff.

Clint grabbed a towel and started drying himself. When he finally did meet the local law he wanted to be dry, and dressed.

FOURTEEN

"Found this in one of their pockets," the sheriff said, holding one of the posters out to Clint.

"No thanks," he said. "I've got one."

They were in the sheriff's office. The three bodies had been removed to the undertaker's, and Clint and the sheriff had gone to the lawman's office, after he relieved Clint of his gun. Now they were seated on opposite sides of the sheriff's desk. The lawman set the poster down on the desktop right next to Clint's gun.

"It's an obvious phony," the sheriff said.

"To a lawman, yes," Clint said, "and that's where I'm lucking out."

The sheriff's name was Thorson. Clint had heard someone at the hotel refer to him as "Babe." He assumed it was a nickname, but it certainly didn't come from the man's appearance. He didn't resemble a "babe" or a "baby" in the least. He was a big man in his fifties who looked as if he had once been powerfully built, but the muscles seemed to have melted and slipped down into his belly. His skin, though, was pale and had a healthy glow to it, and Clint wondered if this was where the nickname came from. This was certainly not a man who spent a great deal of time in the sun.

"I'm gonna send some telegrams," Thorson said, "but I'll have to hold your gun until I get some answers."

"No."

"What?"

"You know who I am, Sheriff."

"I know who you are, Adams."

"Then you know that even if this poster existed I couldn't walk out of here without my gun," Clint said. "You have to either give it back, or lock me up. If I go out on the street without a gun, I'm as good as dead."

"Don't kid me, Adams," Thorson said. "You must have another gun in your saddlebags."

"I'd be dead before I ever got to it."

Thorson sat back in his chair, making it creak, and studied Clint.

"You're right, of course," he said, finally, "and since I don't think you lured three men into the hotel so you could attack them from your bath, I'm going to give you your gun back."

"Thank you," Clint said, reaching for it. Before he could grab it, though, the lawman put a beefy hand on it.

"You got to promise me," Thorson said, "that you ain't gonna kill nobody else in town."

"I promise you," Clint said, "that I won't kill anyone who isn't trying to kill me."

The two men locked eyes, and then Thorson removed his hand from the gun so Clint could reclaim it.

"I guess that's the best I'm gonna do right now," the sheriff said.

Clint strapped on his gun but did not leave the sheriff's office just yet.

"I'm trying to track down the origin of that poster,

Sheriff," he explained, "and that means finding somebody who's passing them out."

"Well," Thorson said, "I know the posters showed up here a few weeks ago, but I never saw who was handing them out."

"I'll need to go around town and ask some questions."

"That sounds kind of risky to me, Adams, considerin' what happened today—and considerin' that you just got here."

"I know," Clint said, "but it's got to be done. I've been going from town to town getting descriptions, and right now it seems like I'm looking for half a dozen different men."

"More than likely the same man with half a dozen different descriptions," Thorson said.

"You're right about that."

Thorson sighed.

"Well, all right, Adams," he said, "go and ask your questions. I'll try to make sure nobody else tries to bushwack you while you're eatin' or sleepin' or doin' your business."

"I appreciate that, Sheriff."

"But if somebody does end up shootin' you dead," the lawman added, "don't come blamin' me."

"You got my word on that, Sheriff."

FIFTEEN

Clint left the sheriff's office and went to the nearest saloon. If you are a stranger in town and you need to ask questions your best bet is always a bartender. If they don't know the answer they usually know who does.

He entered the Wild Horse Saloon and walked to the bar. The place was half full and nobody paid him much mind. Either the word hadn't gotten around about the shooting, or strangers didn't attract that much attention in this town. And if there was a man in the saloon with a poster in his pocket he hadn't yet taken a good look at Clint.

"Beer," he said, and the bartender wasted no time in making one appear at his elbow. Clint already had the poster out. "Ever seen this before?"

As an answer the man reached beneath the bar, pulled out a stack of them and slapped them down on the bar.

"Now how'd you manage that?" Clint asked.

"I been takin' them away from my customers."

"Why's that?"

"Well, one because they're phony."

"How can you tell?"

"I've seen enough of them to know."

57

"What's two?"

"Huh?"

"You said 'one, because they're phony.' What's two?"

"I don't want my customers gettin' shot up."

"Didn't work earlier."

"You musta talked to the sheriff, Mr. Adams," the bartender said. "By now you know those boys weren't local."

As a matter of fact the sheriff *had* been able to tell him that much.

"You recognize me from the poster?" Clint asked.

"It's a good likeness," the man said, "but I seen you before."

"When? Where?"

"Jericho City, Nevada," the man said.

"I've been there."

"I was a deputy there when you were there."

"That had to be ten years ago."

"You ain't changed much."

"Have you?"

"We didn't meet," the man said. "You wouldn't recognize me, anyway, but yeah, I changed."

"How?"

"I'm a lot thinner," the man said. "Gettin' yer insides shot up will do that to ya. I don't each much, no more."

"Sorry to hear it."

"I got out of the law business after that and into the bartending business," the man said.

"What's your name?"

"Wendell Tibbs," the man said, extending his hand. Clint studied Tibbs as they shook. The man looked to be in his forties, but it was more likely he was ten years younger than that. He'd obviously led a hard life.

"I don't suppose you saw whoever was passing these posters out, did you?" Clint asked.

"As a matter of fact," Tibbs said, "I did."

Clint's heart skipped a beat. He was excited. A description from a bartender, and an ex-lawman to boot, would be worth more than any he'd gotten so far.

"What'd he look like?"

"A dude," Tibbs said. "Nice suit, a gambler's suit, but he wasn't no gambler."

That matched a couple of descriptions he'd gotten of a man who looked like a gambler.

"How'd you know that?"

"Feller tried to sit in on a poker game to pass out his posters," Tibbs said. "Didn't know an ace from a deuce."

"What else can you tell me?"

Tibbs leaned on the bar.

"Lemme think," he said. "I been waiting for you to pass this way so's I could tell ya this."

"What made you think I would?"

"Somebody put out a poster of me I'd be riding to hell and back to try and find out who it was."

Somebody down the bar wanted a drink so bad they were waving both hands.

"Hold on a sec."

Tibbs went to the other end of the bar to serve two men, one of whom had been waving his arms. Soon there were raised voices from that end of the bar, attracting Clint's attention.

"I said I want a drink for me and my frien'," the waving man was saying.

"And I said I got to see your money," Tibbs replied. "No money, no drink."

"You sonofa—" the man started, but his friend grabbed his arm.

"Never mind, Dan. Let's go someplace else."

Tibbs started back toward Clint, who took his eyes from the men to watch the bartender, but then peripherally he saw a familiar move as the first man went for his gun and drew it.

"I wanna drink!" he shouted, bringing his gun to bear on the bartender's back.

"Look out!" Clint shouted. "Don't."

The last thing he wanted was for Tibbs to be killed, backshot by a drunk, for more than one reason.

The drunk, startled by Clint's shout, pulled the trigger. Clint drew and fired before the man could pull it again. The shot hit the man in the chest and he fell into his friend's arms.

Tibbs, struck from behind by the bullet, was propelled into a bunch of bottles behind the bar, and slid down to the floor to lie in a puddle of mixed whiskey.

"Goddamn it!" Clint shouted, and vaulted over the bar.

SIXTEEN

"How is he?" Clint asked Sheriff Thorson.

"He's alive," Thorson said, "but he ain't gonna be talkin' anytime soon."

Once again Clint was seated across from Sheriff Thorson with his gun on the desk.

"I thought we had a deal," the lawman said. "You weren't going to kill anyone who wasn't trying to kill you."

"He was going to shoot Tibbs."

"Maybe," Thorson said. "His partner says he only pulled the trigger because you startled him, that there was no need to kill him."

"I had no way of knowing that," Clint said. "I couldn't afford to take that chance, even if it was true."

"Why not?"

"Tibbs has some information I need."

"Ah," Thorson said, "about the posters."

"That's right."

Thorson studied Clint for a few moments, then leaned forward and pushed his gun across the desk to him.

"Thanks."

"The next time you shoot someone," Thorson said, "you better have a bullet in you, first."

Clint stood and holstered his gun.

"You're always asking me to make hard promises."

Clint got directions to the doctor's office from Thorson before leaving his office, and he headed directly there.

The doctor's name was Evans, and according to Thorson he was a pretty good sawbones. As Clint entered the man's office he saw a white-haired gent coming through another door. He assumed that the other room was the doctor's surgery.

"Doctor Evans?"

"That's right. Can I help you?"

"My name is Clint Adams," Clint said. "How's Mr. Tibbs?"

"Ah, you're the man who kept him from being killed?"

"That's how I look at it, anyway," Clint said. "Some people have other ideas about the way things happened."

"Well," Evans said, "I don't understand any of that. Tibbs was shot high, near the right shoulder. He's in shock, and he's sustained some ligament damage, but the wound is not life-threatening—thanks to me."

"Sheriff Thorson told me you were pretty good."

"Nice of Babe to say so."

"Babe," Clint said. "You're the second person I've heard call him that. Where'd that nickname come from?"

"Nickname?" Evans asked. "That's his first name, his *real* name."

"Babe?"

"That's it."

Clint shook his head.

"There's got to be a story behind that one."

"If there is," Evans said, "he's not talking about it—and I'm his best friend."

"I see."

"Anyway," Evans said, "I'll keep Tibbs here overnight, but tomorrow arrangements will have to be made to take him home."

"I guess I can take care of that," Clint said, "except . . ."

"Except what?"

"I don't know where he lives."

"Well," Evans said, "he owns the saloon, and he lives above it. If you go and talk to any of the girls who work for him, they can help you."

"The girls?"

"Saloon girls," Evans said. "He's got three working for him. Laurie, Bette and Cassandra. Three nice gals."

"Laurie, Bette and Cassandra."

"Right."

"I'll go and talk to them."

As Clint turned the doctor said, "By the way, who's taking care of my bill?"

Clint stopped with his hand on the doorknob, and said, "I guess that would be me."

Evans smiled and said, "I'll have it ready tomorrow."

Clint nodded, and went out.

SEVENTEEN

Clint went back to the saloon, which was still open and running despite the condition of its owner. There was another man behind the bar, and the place had filled up some since he was there last. The mess behind the bar had been cleaned up and it looked like business as usual.

He also saw that there were three girls working the floor now, where there had been none before. He went to the bar and knew that he was not going unnoticed as he had the first time he'd walked in. Apparently, there were still some patrons there who had also been present during the shooting.

When he got to the bar he said, "Beer."

"Comin' up."

The bartender brought it over and looked at him.

"You're the fella helped out Tibbs earlier today, ain't ya?"

"That's not the way a lot of folks look at it," Clint said. "Seems I may have overreacted."

"The way I hear it, he's still alive because of you," the man said. "He is still alive, ain't he?"

"He is."

"Well then," the bartender said, "you'll be drinkin' on the house until I hear him say different."

"Thanks. Listen, are these girls, uh, Laurie, Bette and uh—"

"Cassandra," the barman said. "Yep, that's them. Why?"

"The doctor said they might be able to help me with some information."

"You want me to introduce you?"

"Sure, why not?"

"All at once," the man asked, "or one at a time."

"One at a time would probably work better."

"Stick around, then," the bartender said.

"I've got no place else to go tonight."

"By the way," the man said, "the name's Maker. I work for Tibbs when he needs help behind the bar."

"First or last?"

"Just Maker."

"Nice to meet you, Maker."

The two men shook hands. Maker looked as if he could have been forty or fifty, give or take a few years either way. He was short, but built solidly, and his handshake reflected that. His sleeves were pushed up to his elbows and he had wiry black hair up and down his arms, and on the back of his hands.

"I'll gets the girls over here one at a time over the next hour or so. After all, they got to work."

"I understand," Clint said. "Like I said, I've got no-where else to go."

Laurie was brunette, in her early thirties the oldest of the girls—or women. She was tall, slender, with pale skin and pretty blue eyes.

"How is Wendell?" she asked.

"He'll be fine," Clint said. "He'll need some help getting from the doctor's office to where he lives."

She pointed to the ceiling and said, "That'd be upstairs."

"Can you get some men to carry him over here on a stretcher?" he asked.

"I can arrange that," she said. "We got to thank you for helpin' him—me and the other girls, I mean."

"Actually, I was trying to keep him alive for selfish reasons."

"What reasons?"

"The posters he keeps behind the bar?"

Her mouth dropped open.

"That's you on the poster?"

"That's me."

"Then that would make you . . ."

"Clint Adams."

"The Gunsmith!"

"That's right."

"Wow," she said. "I never met a legend before."

"That's okay," he said. "I never wanted to be one. Anyway, can you tell me anything about the man who was giving out the posters?"

"Gee," she said, "I know there was someone giving them out, but I can't remember who it was."

"Do you think the other girls might remember?"

"Maybe," she said, "but you'd have to ask them. Do you want me to bring them over?"

"No," Clint said. "Maker is going to introduce me to them."

"That's good," she said. "Maybe we can talk again later."

"I'd like that, Laurie. Thanks."

She smiled, turned and flounced off back to work.

Bette was a blonde with a big, solid body that threatened to bust the seams of her dress. Her skin was also pale, her mouth full, her chin almost plump. She was in her mid-twenties, and Clint wondered how old she'd be before her weight started to get out of control. At the moment, though, she was every man's dream of a bed partner, drunk or sober—the men, that is.

She asked Clint how Tibbs was, flirted with him and answered his questions. She also could not remember what the man with the posters looked like.

Clint watched her walk away to return to work and ordered another beer for his dry throat.

Cassandra had red hair, which was long but—unlike the other girls, who also had long hair—she wore it up to reveal a graceful neck. She was a bigger girl than Laurie, but certainly not as big as Bette. Tibbs seemed to have hired three girls of varying sizes, perhaps for variety. She was also younger than the other two, probably in her early twenties.

"No," she said, shaking her head, "I don't remember that man who was handing out posters, but maybe that's because he didn't hand them out to women."

"You're probably right," Clint said. "But you did see them?"

"Of yes," she said, but she didn't seem to realize that the drawing on the paper was him. Neither did Bette. That was good. He'd already dealt with that question once, with Laurie. He was grateful not to have to do it again.

"Are you sure Wendell is okay?" she asked.

"Yes," Clint said, "the doctor says he's fine, and he can come home tomorrow. Laurie's going to find me some men to help him over here."

"Yeah," Cassandra said, "that Laurie, she's real helpful."

"Thanks for your help, Cassandra—"

"You can call me Cass," she said, "and any time you need help, you just ask me, you hear?"

"I hear."

As she walked away he grabbed his beer and finished it off. All three girls had a way of making a man's mouth go dry.

EIGHTEEN

Clint stayed at the saloon for a few more hours, watching the action take place around him. The only gambling being done was a couple of private poker games that were going on, which he didn't want to sit in on. The girls— now that they knew who he was—kept coming back to give him some attention, and by splitting him among them, he spent very little time not talking to one of them—and when he did, he was talking to Maker.

"The girls like you," Maker said.

"Well, they think I saved the life of the man who pays them," Clint reasoned.

"I think the same thing," Maker said, "and I don't like you."

Clint looked at him.

"I mean," the bartender added, "I don't *not* like you, but I don't like you the way they do."

"And what way is that?"

"The way that makes three girls fight over one man."

"I don't think so," Clint said. "They just met me."

"That don't matter," Maker said. "You're a man, you oughta know that."

Clint did know that. He'd ended up in bed with women

71

minutes after meeting them before, so it was no surprise when a woman took to him right away, and vice versa— but three at one time?

"Three at one time," Maker said, as if reading Clint's mind. "Ain't that every man's dream?"

"Maybe," Clint said.

"You wouldn't like to have three women at once?"

"I like concentrating on one thing at a time," Clint said. "That includes women."

The bartender stared at him, then said, "You've had three women at one time, ain't ya?"

"Well . . . once," Clint said.

The bartender shook his head and walked away.

It was getting late and Clint decided to turn in before he got somebody else mad at him.

He left the saloon very carefully, remembering what had happened in Limestone. He stood just outside the batwing doors for a few moments, letting his eyes adjust from the inside to the outside. He saw no one lurking in the shadows and started for the hotel, careful to go wide every time he encountered an alley.

As he stepped up onto the boardwalk in front of the hotel he saw a man get up from a chair in front of the window.

"There you are," Sheriff Thorson said.

"You waiting for me, Sheriff?"

"Watching out for you, is more like it," Thorson said. "Just wanted to make sure you got tucked in safe and sound tonight, without nobody goin' after that phony reward money."

"Well," Clint said. "I must say I'm touched, Sheriff."

"Don't be," Thorson said. "I just don't want no more trouble in my town, Adams."

"Can't say I blame you, Sheriff," Clint said. "I'm turning in right now, as a matter of fact."

"Good," Thorson said. "I'll just hang around out here a while longer to make sure nobody follows you up."

"I'm much obliged, Sheriff," Clint said, "even if you *are* just doing your job."

"Good night, Adams."

"Good night, Sheriff."

Clint went inside and up the stairs to his room. He opened the door to his room with gun in hand, but the room was empty. He thought again about the sheriff sitting down in the dark, waiting for him to come back to the hotel. That was a little above and beyond a lawman's job, he thought. He wondered if maybe Thorson himself was thinking about that reward. But the lawman had seen the poster, and knew that it was a phony. There was little chance that he'd try something himself.

Nevertheless, Clint grabbed a straight-backed wooden chair from near the window and jammed it under the doorknob, then took the pitcher and basin from the dresser and set them on the window ledge. Alarms set, he laid down on the bed with his gun hanging on the bedpost within easy reach, and went to sleep.

NINETEEN

To Clint's everlasting satisfaction the night went by un-eventfully. His booby traps were still in place and the chair was still solidly planted beneath the doorknob. It had occurred to him during the night that the sheriff might have been waiting for him just to make sure he was in his room, maybe for his own knowledge, or to pass the information on to someone else. If the lawman was after the reward he would have to bring someone else in on it, because he couldn't have claimed it himself.

But it was morning now and nothing had happened, so if the sheriff had any plans to try and pick up the reward he hadn't chosen to make a move last night.

Clint got dressed and went downstairs to have some breakfast. All he needed to do today was see if Tibbs was awake and able to speak. If he was, and he got the de-scription he needed from the saloon owner, he'd be able to leave Grateful behind. He never liked hanging around a town if he had been forced to kill a man, and here he had been forced to kill four.

He took breakfast in the hotel dining room, then walked over to the doctor's office to see about Tibbs.

"Morning, Doc," he said, as he entered.

"Oh, good morning, Mr. Adams," the doctor said. "What can I do for you?"

"I was wondering if Tibbs was awake."

"Well," Evans said, "he *was* when they took him out."

"What?"

"He's been moved to his saloon," Evans said. "I thought you'd know that."

"How would I know that?"

"Well, I guess I just assumed that you'd arranged it."

"I'm a stranger in town, Doc," Clint said. "I doubt that I could arrange anything. It must have been the people who work for him."

"I guess so," Evans said. "Anyway, they came for him real early and he was awake when they carried him out. I guess if you want to see him you'll have to go over to his place."

"I'll do that, Doc," Clint said. "Thanks."

Clint left the doctor's office, wondering what the big rush had been. It had to have been *real* early when they came over to get him. Why couldn't they have waited until later in the morning, or in the afternoon?

He walked to the saloon but found the front doors locked. He wondered if anyone would hear him if he pounded on the doors, then assumed that someone would. After all, they had to be awake to come and get him. He knocked on the doors, waited, and pounded on them. Finally, someone arrived and opened them. It was Laurie, the brunette. She stood with her hands on her hips, looking at him.

"Well, somebody wants a drink real early."

"I'm here to see Tibbs, Laurie," Clint said. "Is he awake?"

"I think so," she said. "At least, he was a few minutes ago."

"Can I see him?"

"I don't see why not. Come on in."

He entered and she locked the doors behind him. Maker was behind the bar, apparently getting set up for the day.

"Mornin'," he said.

"Good morning, Maker."

"Here to see Tibbs?"

"That's right."

"Can I get you somethin' first?" Maker asked. "A drink?"

"It's too early."

"Coffee, then?"

Clint hesitated, then said, "Coffee would be good."

"I'll go and find out if he's awake," Laurie said.

"Okay," Clint said, and approached the bar. He accepted the cup of coffee the bartender handed him, and tasted it.

"Whataya think?" Maker asked.

"Pretty good," Clint said, even though it wasn't. "You people sure got up early to get Tibbs over here."

"Figured he'd rather be in his own bed," Maker said. "I got a coupla fellas to go over there with me and carry him here."

"How's he doing?"

"Pretty good," Maker said. "Was talkin' up a storm, asking how we did last night, and all. That's a good sign."

"I guess so," Clint said. He put the coffee cup down, hoping the man wouldn't ask him about it.

He heard footsteps on the stairs, looked up and saw Bette, the blonde, coming down.

"Good morning," she said. "Tibbs is awake and waiting for you, Mr. Adams."

"Thanks, Bette," he said, and then to the bartender, "thanks for the coffee, Maker."

"Sure," Maker said, "any time."

"This way," Bette said, and led the way to the stairs.

Clint watched her behind sway enticingly as he followed her up the steps and then down the hall to a door at the end. She opened it and went in, beckoning Clint to follow her.

"You have a visitor, Tibbs," she said, loudly.

Clint came in behind her and looked at the man in the bed. He was lying on his back with his eyes closed.

"I thought you said he was awake," Clint said, in a low voice.

"Oh, he is," Bette said. "Just go over and talk to him. He'll open his eyes."

Clint walked over to the bed and looked down at the man. It only took him a second to realize that Tibbs would never open his eyes again. Then he heard a familiar sound behind him, the sound of the hammer being drawn back on a revolver.

Then he heard it again.

And a third time.

TWENTY

"Stand very still," a woman said to him.

"I'm not moving," he said.

"Raise your hands."

He did as he was told.

"All three of you are here?"

"Yes," Laurie said.

"With guns?"

"Yes," Cassandra said.

"Pointing at you," Bette said.

"I'm just going to turn my head to make sure," he said.

"Go ahead," Laurie said.

He swiveled his head around and saw all three women holding revolvers on him. Cassandra's was a little too big for her and she was holding it with two hands. The other two women were holding their guns in one hand, but Laurie was the only one who looked as if she had ever held a gun before.

"How long has he been dead?" Clint asked. "Right from the start?" Which would mean the doctor had been in on this.

"No," Laurie said. "He died during the night."

"So a dead man was carried over here?"

"That's right," Laurie said.

That meant the doctor and Maker, the bartender, had been in on it, but neither of them were up here holding a gun on him. The women were in charge here. Or, at least, Laurie was.

"This your idea, Laurie?" he asked.

"What if it is?"

"It's a big mistake."

"Why?"

"Because the poster is a fake," he said. "The reward is not real."

"That's what you say," Laurie replied.

"Ask the sheriff . . . or is he in on this, too?"

"No," Laurie said. "Not him."

"Then ask him."

"He'll back your story."

"Why would he?" Clint asked. "We're not friends. We just met yesterday. Why would he back my story if I'm lying?"

"Because," Laurie said, "you're both men."

"What about the doc and Maker?" he asked. "Aren't they men?"

"Yes," she said, "that's what made it easy to get them to go along."

"Ah," Clint said, "who slept with who?"

"Why does that matter?"

"If I'm going to die," Clint said, "I'd just like to satisfy my curiosity."

There was hesitation, then Laurie said, "Bette stayed with the Doc, and Cassandra went with Maker."

"And are they getting any of the money?"

"They think they are."

"Ah, I see," he said. "You're going to double-cross them."

No answer.

"And kill them, too?"

"That won't be necessary," she said.

"Just me, huh?"

"That's right."

"You're going to be real disappointed," Clint said, "when you find out you killed me for no reason at all."

"Laurie—" Bette said.

"Quiet, Bette," Laurie snapped.

"But what if he's telling the truth?" Bette asked.

"I said be still!"

"What if he is, Laurie?" Cassandra asked.

"Not you, too, Cassie."

"I'm just wondering," Cassie said. "After all, I never killed anybody before."

"It's not a pretty sight, Cassie," Clint said. "All that blood."

"Shut up!" Laurie said.

"Bette?" Clint asked. "You ever kill a man?"

"N-no," Bette said.

"That leaves you, Laurie."

"I have killed a man," she said. "Back east, before I came here."

"With a gun?"

"Yes."

Clint believed her. She was the one he had to worry about in this threesome.

"It's time for you to take off your gun belt," she said to him.

"Mmm, I don't think so."

"What?"

"I can't do that."

"Why not?"

"You'll kill me."

"We're going to kill you, anyway."

"That's my point," he said. "Why take off my gun if you're going to shoot me, anyway? I might as well take one or two of you with me."

"What?" Bette asked.

"Laurie," Cassie said, "make him take it off."

"I'm going to turn and draw my gun, ladies," he said, calmly. "Any of you who are pointing a gun at me when I do will die. It's as simple as that."

"He's bluffing," Laurie said. "Don't listen to him."

"What have I got to gain by bluffing?" he asked. "No, my only hope is to draw and see how many of you I can kill before one of you kills me."

"Make him take it *off!*" Cassie shouted.

"I'm going to count to three, ladies," Clint said.

"One . . . two . . ."

TWENTY-ONE

"Before I get to three," he asked, "would anyone like to say something?"

"Laurie—" Bette said.

"Go ahead and count," Laurie said to Clint, and he could tell she was going to pull the trigger.

He drew his gun faster than their eyes could follow and trained it right on Laurie, whose eyes widened in shock. The situation had gone from them having three guns trained on him with his hands in the air, to his having a gun trained right back at them—at *her.*

"Now it really is your call, Laurie," he said. "My first bullet is for you."

"No!" Cassie shouted, and dropped her gun to the floor.

"Cass—"

"Me, too," Bette said, and dropped hers. "The money ain't worth getting you killed over."

"Laurie?" Clint asked.

She stared at him, wet her lips, and then her shoulders slumped and her arm dropped to her side, as if the gun had suddenly gained fifty pounds. She still held it, pointing at the floor.

"Drop it, Laurie," he said, quietly.

She didn't. She just continued to stare at the floor.

"Do it, Laurie," Bette said.

"Please, Laurie!" Cassie said.

She looked at her two friends, and then her fingers opened and her gun fell to the floor.

"That's good," Clint said. He moved quickly, stepping to them and kicking each gun under the bed. That done, he holstered his own.

"What are you gonna do with us?" Bette asked.

"Nothing," he said.

"Nothing?" Cassandra asked.

"That's right."

"Why?" Laurie asked. "I would have killed you."

"You're just three more people who believed a lie," he said.

"You mean . . ." Bette said.

"I was telling the truth, ladies," he said. "That poster is no good."

Cassandra glared at Laurie and said, "You almost made us kill him for nothing!" and stormed out of the room.

Bette put her hand on Laurie's shoulder, then left the room, running after Cassandra.

"She's right," Laurie said. "I-I'm sorry. I just—I just wanted to get away from here."

"Why?" he asked.

"Look at him," she said, indicating Tibbs, lying in his bed. "He's dead. He treated us good. What's gonna happen to us now that he's gone?"

"I don't know," Clint said. "Maybe the new owner will treat you good, too."

"I doubt that," she said, shaking her head. "Tibbs was the only man who ever treated us well. Where would we find another?"

"Who is the new owner?" he asked.

"I don't know."

"Did if ever occur to you," he asked, "that it might be you?"

"Me?"

"Or the three of you," Clint said. "Is there a lawyer in town?"

"Yes."

"Maybe he has Tibbs's will."

"I-I never thought of that," she said. "I just assumed he'd leave it to another man, like Maker."

"Would that be so bad?" he asked. "He seems okay."

"He got what he wanted last night," she said. "If he took over one of us would have to sleep with him every night."

"Why is that?"

"Because," she said, slowly, as if speaking to a child, "he's a man."

"Well," Clint said, "maybe before you decide to do something that would drastically change your life you should find out who owns the saloon."

"Yes," she said, "you're right." She lifted her head and looked at him, ashamed. "Can you ever forgive me?"

"Forget it," he said. "My beef is with whoever is circulating that phony poster." He looked down at Tibbs. "What about him?"

"We'll have him buried today," she said. "I'll talk to the undertaker."

"And do me a favor," he said.

"What's that?"

"Talk to Doc and Maker," he said. "Make them understand that there's no reward?"

"I'll tell them," she said, "but they don't care. They each got what they wanted last night."

"It'll just make me feel better."

"Okay."

As she turned to leave he said, "Laurie?"

"Yes?"

"Tibbs was going to give me the description of the man who gave him the poster." He looked down at the dead man. "Obviously, that's not going to happen now. Can you help me with that?"

"I'm really sorry, Mr. Adams," she said. "I'd like to help you, especially after what we almost did, but I just don't know."

"Okay," he said, "that's okay." He looked down at Tibbs, a man who had seemed poised to give him some information he really could have used. "I'll just keep looking."

TWENTY-TWO

Amanda Coates looked up as William Hyde, her assistant, entered her office. This was her home office, rather than one of the many offices she kept in businesses that she owned around the city.

"William," she said. "What news?"

"Not much, I'm afraid," William Hyde said.

"He's still alive?"

"As far as we know."

"And the posters?"

"We've saturated the area with them," Hyde said. "We do know that some attempts were made on him, but that none were successful."

Amanda raised her right hand and touched the ruined left side of her face. The flesh was shiny and scarred from her cheekbone to her chin, and there was a slight droop to her left eye. When she left the house she usually wore a veil to hide her face from prying or curious eyes. William Hyde, her assistant for several years, was the only one who ever saw her face uncovered—he and the servants in her house.

Hyde was in his thirties and performed a variety of services for Amanda Coates—services she could not get from anyone else. At forty, except for the scarred face, she was a perfectly healthy woman, with certain needs which had to be attended to. Hyde was paid very well to see to all these needs.

At the present time she had a burning need to see Clint Adams dead.

"It will take some time," Hyde said, "but he will fall."

She dropped her hand from her face and looked up at Hyde.

"I don't know if I can wait that long, William," she said. "I just don't know."

William Hyde was generaly known to all as a hard man, but when it came to Amanda Coates he was not hard at all.

"What would you have me do, Ma'am?"

She looked up at him, making no move to hide the ruination of what had once been a beautiful face. What she did not know was that to him her face was still very beautiful.

"Can you hurry things along, William?"

"I can try."

"I know you, William," she said, with what he hoped was affection. "You can do more than try."

"Yes, Ma'am."

"I don't want this to drag on."

"Yes, Ma'am."

"I need it to be over."

He backed toward the door and said, "I'll see what I can do, Mrs. Coates. I'll do my best."

"I know you will, William," she said. "I know you will."

TWENTY-THREE

In a town called River Bend, Clint received two telegrams that sent him to Denver. One was from Rick Hartman, telling him that a bunch of the posters had shown up in Denver. The other telegram was from his friend in Denver, Talbot Roper, the best private detective in the business. He also advised Clint to come to Denver, not only because the posters were there, but because he thought he could help. Either was reason enough to go to Denver, but both combined with Roper's offer of help made the trip imperative.

When he rode into Denver he went directly to the Denver House Hotel, which was his regular place to stay when he was in town. Most of the doormen, bellmen or clerks who had been there for any period of time knew him. The same went for the liveryman who manned the hotel livery.

"Welcome back, Mr. Adams," liveryman Hal Sykes said. "That sure is one pretty horse, but it ain't Duke."

"No, it's not Duke," Clint said, dismounting. He'd had to break this news to liverymen all over the West. "I had to put Duke out to pasture."

"Ol' Duke? Out in the pasture?"

89

"That's right."

"If that don't beat all," the man said, taking off his hat and brushing back his white hair with his hand. "I thought that gelding was gonna go on forever." He replaced the hat.

"That's what I thought, too, for a while," Clint said, "but none of us go on forever, Hal."

"Where'd you get this one, then?" Sykes asked. "Handsome animal. What is he, anyway?"

"This is Eclipse," Clint said. "He's a Darley Arabian from Europe. He was a gift to me from P. T. Barnum."

"From who?"

"A friend," Clint said. Barnum would be crushed to know he wasn't known all over the West. "Never mind. Just take good care of him, will you?"

Sykes accepted the reins and said, "I'll treat him like he was Duke hisself."

"That's a good idea," Clint said. "You do that."

"How long you gonna be stayin', Mr. Adams?"

"Don't know, Hal," Clint said. "I've got some business in town that could take days, or weeks. I just don't know."

"Well," Sykes said, "that don't matter none. You just rest easy knowin' your new horse is in good hands."

"I know he is, thanks," Clint said. He collected his gear and walked around to the hotel to check in.

"Mr. Adams," the desk clerk greeted, "how nice to have you back, sir."

Clint wasn't sure of the man's name so he said, "Thanks, nice to be back," and signed in.

"There's a message here for you," the clerk said, handing it to him.

"Thank you."

He felt badly about not remembering the man's name, because the man had obviously remembered that he liked carrying his own things to his room and didn't offer him a bell hop.

Clint went to his room, which traditionally was on the second floor of the three-story hotel. His window overlooked the front of the street, but there were no balconies or ledges outside. He dropped his gear on the bed and opened the message. It was from Talbot Roper, saying he would meet Clint in the lobby at seven P.M. It was now four, which gave him time to have a bath and a couple of hours' rest.

He dug a fresh shirt out of his saddlebags and went downstairs to arrange for the bath.

Clint was in the lobby at seven P.M. when Talbot Roper came walking in. Roper, once a Pinkerton who could not conform to Allan Pinkerton's way of doing things, had gone on to become one of the most successful private detectives in the country. Clint counted him among his closest friends, along with Luke Short, Bat Masterson and Rick Hartman.

"Clint," Roper said, with his hand outstretched.

"Tal."

The two men shared a warm handshake—the two-handed kind that men who really like each other employ.

"I see you got my message," Roper said. "Dinner here all right?"

"Always," Clint said. He liked the food at the Denver House quite a bit.

The two men walked together to the dining room, where Clint was greeted warmly. They were shown to a table from which they could see the entire room.

"Steaks?" the waiter asked.

Clint looked at Roper, who said, "Definitely."

"I'll bring the coffee," the waiter said, and left.

"You've got them trained here," Roper said.

Clint didn't mention that Roper had waiters and waitresses in restaurants all over the city just as trained.

"How are you holding up?" Roper asked his friend.

"Considering there's an even bigger target painted on my back than usual," Clint said, "I think I'm doing quite well."

"Well, I guess you're used to being a target, but not one with a price on your head."

The waiter returned with the coffee, poured them each a cup and left.

"What can you tell me, Tal?"

"When I first saw the posters I knew they were phony."

"You recognized that by looking at them?"

Roper smiled at Clint and said, "I know you, Clint, that's how I knew they were phony."

"I appreciate that, Tal."

"But yes," Roper went on, "I could tell from looking at them that they were phony. There was no contact for the reward, and no indication as to what you were wanted for."

"That's what surprises me the most," Clint said. "Can't people see that even if they were to kill me there's nothing to tell them who to get the reward from?"

"All people see is that number," Roper said. "The twenty-five hundred dollars."

"Okay," Clint said, "so you knew they were phony. Go on."

"I decided to try and find out where they came from."

"And how did you do that?"

"Contacts," Roper said. "I have contacts all over the country, Clint. I started sending out telegrams, and kept sending them out until answers started coming back."

"And you got the answer?"

"I got the answer," Roper said. He leaned forward and asked, "Does the name Amanda Coates ring a bell."

Clint stared at his friend for a few moments, then said, "Oh my God."

TWENTY-FOUR

"You know her?" Roper asked.

"I knew her and her husband, once."

"And what happened?"

"He died in a fire," Clint said. "She survived, but her face was burned."

"There's more to the story than that."

"Much more."

The waiter came with their steaks, then, and they paused long enough for him to set their plates down and ask if they needed anything else.

"All right, then," Roper said. "Let's hear it."

Clint told him the story.

It happened several years earlier, while Clint was still riding Duke, his big black gelding. He and Duke rode into the town of Brown's Fork, Missouri. He was there to see a friend named Ben Coates, and to meet his new wife, Amanda. Actually, she wasn't so new; they had been married for three years or so, but Clint had never met her before. In fact, he hadn't seen Ben Coates since well before he'd gotten married. Since then though, he'd settled down and had a ranch with Amanda.

Clint remembered Coates as a hellraiser, a man who didn't often make the right decision when he could just as well make the wrong one. Now that he was settled down, though, it had to be due to Amanda. Leaves it to a good woman to settle down a wild man every time.

Maybe.

He stopped in Brown's Fork to get a drink at the saloon before continuing on to the Coates ranch. What he didn't realize was that Ben Coates would be waiting for him in town. In fact, he was in the saloon when Clint entered.

"What the hell are you doing here?" Clint asked.

Coates smiled the biggest smile Clint could ever remember seeing on a man.

"I knew you'd stop here for a drink, and I didn't want you to get lost," Coates said. "One drink and then you're comin' out to the ranch to meet Amanda."

"That was my plan."

"Well, I'm here to make sure you stick to it."

They both turned toward the bar and ordered two beers. Coates was about thirty-five at that time, and even though he'd turned to ranching he was still wearing as gun. As Clint recalled, he was pretty good with a gun, though certainly no gunman.

As the bartender brought them their beers Clint was about to speak when another man's voice called out, "Is that him?"

Clint turned in the direction of the voice, to see if it was referring to him.

"I asked you is that him?" the man said. "Is that the Gunsmith you been talkin' about?"

"Ignore him," Coates said. "He and his buddies are looking for trouble."

Clint looked at Coates. Bragging in a saloon that Clint Adams was coming to visit him was the kind of thing the old Ben Coates would have done. Maybe the love of a good woman hadn't changed him all that much, after all.

"Ben—"

"I might have mentioned you a couple of times," Coates said. "It's no big deal."

"Come on, boy," the spokesman said, "let's meet up with this here friend of Ben Coates's the Gunsmith."

The man speaking was about thirty, wearing worn trail clothes and an equally worn gun and holster. The only way a weapon got into that condition was if the owner made a habit of using it.

Behind him were three other men, similarly dressed and outfitted.

"You know these fellas, Ben?"

"I'm acquainted with them, yeah," Coates said. Then he raised his voice. "Big mouths, the lot of them."

"Izat so?" the spokesman asked. "Why don't you tell your friend the truth, Coates?"

"Don't listen to them," Coates said, trying not to pay any attention.

"Tell him that you owe us money, huh?" the man said. "Lost money in a poker game you ain't got? Promised us a chance—"

"I promised you nothin'!" Coates roared suddenly, turning on the three men. "But I'll tell you what you're gonna get. You're gonna get a chance at the Gunsmith, here, but with me by his side. Get it?"

The four men fanned out and others in the saloon ducked for cover. Clint turned to face the four men head on.

"Look, boys," Clint said, "I don't know what the beef is, but I just got to town. I haven't even tasted my beer yet. I'm really not in the mood to kill anybody, right now. Why don't you all just think it over and maybe we can take up where we left off tomorrow, huh?"

Clint stared the four men down, aware that Coates was standing at his side, his hand down by his gun.

"What's your name?" Clint asked the spokesman.

"Huh?"

"Your name?"

"Uh, it's Rand."

"You the leader here, Rand?"

"There's no leader," he said. "We're all together—right boys?"

The other three men nodded their agreement, though not vehemently.

"Okay, so you're not the leader, you're just the loudmouth. Is that it?"

"Look, friend," Rand said, "the loudmouth is your friend here. He promised us a chance at you if that would square his debt to us."

Clint looked at Coates.

"Is that true, Ben?"

Coates hesitated, then asked, "What do you think?"

"I think that sounds like something you would have set up a few years ago," Clint said. "I thought maybe being married had changed you. Looks like I might have been wrong."

"Look, Clint," Coates said, "we can talk about this out at my ranch later."

"How much does he owe you boys?" Clint asked.

"All told," Rand said, "two hundred twenty-seven dollars."

"Will you settle for the money?" Clint asked. "Nobody gets killed?"

Rand looked at his friends, who all nodded.

"Sure," Rand said, then, "nobody gets killed."

"Come outside with me," Clint said. "It's in my saddlebags."

Rand looked wary.

"How about you and I go out, Rand, and the others stay here?"

"Two of us with you," Rand said, "and two in here with him."

"Sounds fine," Clint said.

"You're gonna leave me here?" Coates demanded.

"Why not?" Clint asked. "I seem to remember you're good enough with a gun to handle two men. Besides, we'll be right back."

Clint, Rand and one of the other men walked out to Clint's saddlebags, where Clint dug into an emergency fund he had taken to carrying. He handed two hundred and thirty dollars over to Rand.

"A few extra dollars for your trouble," he said. "No need to make change."

"Stiller," Rand said, counting the money, "go in and get the boys."

"Right."

Stiller went inside and came out with the other two. They all backed out, then turned when they realized their backs were to Clint.

"We been paid, boys," Rand said. "Let's move."

The four men walked off down the street as Coates came out of the saloon.

"Well," he said, "I'm glad that's settled. I owe you some money, Clint. Come on out to the house and I'll—"

"I don't think so, Ben."

"What?"

Clint turned to face Coates.

"I thought we were friends."

"We are friends!"

"I forgot what a conniver you were, Ben," Clint said. "You were going to hang me out to dry over a two-hundred-dollar debt."

"I knew you could handle those four," Coates said. "And for sure I knew we could handle them together."

Clint gathered Duke's reins up and mounted the big black gelding.

"You should have paid your debt, Ben," he said, then

turned Duke and rode out of town the way he had come, feeling sad, as if a friend had died.

Or a friendship . . .

"So you never met Amanda Coates?" Roper asked.

"No," Clint said, "I left town and never went back."

"So . . . what happened?"

"Apparently," Clint said, "the four men rode out to Coates's ranch and burned it to the ground, with him in it."

"What did they do that for?" Roper demanded. "They'd been paid."

"I don't know," Clint said. "I just read about it later. I also read that Amanda put the blame on me."

"On you? Why? You bailed her husband out of a debt."

"Apparently, that wasn't the way she heard it," Clint said. "The papers said she blamed me, saying that the four men came out to their ranch looking for me. She said they burned it down when they realized I wasn't there. She said her husband stood with me against them in the saloon, and that I had left him to face them alone later."

"And what happened to her?"

"I heard that she was injured in the fire," Clint said. "I never knew how seriously."

"Well, I guess maybe we know now," Roper said. "Seriously enough to want to get you killed."

TWENTY-FIVE

After dinner Clint and Roper went from the dining room to the bar and ordered a beer each. They stood at the bar and drank it.

"How did you get her name?" Clint asked.

"I have a contact in San Francisco who was around when the posters began circulating," Roper said. "He recognized it as a fake, and responded to a telegram I had sent out for information."

"San Francisco?"

"Apparently," Roper said, "that's where the lady is right now. And there's more."

"How much more?"

"She's a very wealthy woman," Roper said. "Apparently, she's become successful since you last had contact—or almost had contact—with her."

"Successful? In what way?"

"Investments," Roper said. "That's all I can find out, right now. Maybe she and her husband had more assets than you knew about?"

"But he couldn't pay a two hundred-and-twenty-seven-dollar debt," Clint said.

"Couldn't?" Roper asked. "Or simply didn't want to?"

"I don't know."

"You didn't stay around to ask."

"No," Clint said. "I didn't want any part of what he had to offer, at that point."

"Can't say I blame you much," Roper said, "but maybe you wouldn't be in this predicament if you hadn't stormed out of town so quickly back then."

Clint swirled what was left of his beer around the bottom of his mug and said, "You're probably right about that."

"So it looks like you've got no choice in the matter," Roper said.

"No," Clint replied, "I don't. I'll have to head for San Francisco to talk to Amanda Coates personally."

"I'll give you my contact's name," Roper said, "and have him meet you at the train station."

"Thanks."

"One thing, though."

"What's that?"

"He's expensive."

"Ah."

"Nothin' for nothin'," Roper said. "That's his motto."

"I'll keep that in mind," Clint said. "By the way, if he's expensive then I owe you whatever you paid him for—"

"You don't owe me anything," Roper said. "Just come out of this thing alive, that's all I ask."

"Well," Clint said, "at least let me pay for the beer."

"I'll do that," Roper said, putting his empty mug down on the bar. "In fact, since you're buying, I'll even have another."

They had another . . . and another . . . and another, and then Clint thanked Roper, who went on his way while Clint went up to his room. He needed to get some sleep if he was going to catch an early train to San Francisco.

Clint hadn't even thought about Ben and Amanda

Coates since leaving Brown's Fork that day. Not until
he'd read the article in the newspaper about the ranch
being burned down. He recalled now that the article had
described Coates as a "prominent" rancher. Had his friend
done that well for himself that his widow had been able
to relocate to San Francisco after his death, and then im-
prove her fortunes even more? And now she was using
that fortune to exact revenge on him for some unknown
or imagined offense?

But then it wasn't unknown, was it? In that newspaper
article she had placed the blame on him, saying that the
assailants were at their ranch looking for "The Gunsmith,"
and when they discovered that he was not there they had
burned it to the ground.

He had considered it a false accusation then, one made
in haste by a grieving widow—but that could no longer
be the case, now. She'd had plenty of time to think things
over, and she had decided to put a price on his head now,
years after the incident.

Clint was finally going to get to meet Amanda Coates.

In San Francisco two men met outside a bar on the Barbary Coast.

"So?" William Hyde asked.

"It's done," Sam Baker said.

"You sent the telegram to Roper?"

"With the information you paid me to give him, yes,"
Baker said.

"And what have you heard?"

"That Clint Adams is in Denver right at this moment,
having met with Roper," Baker said. "I'm to meet Adams
at the train station when he arrives."

"Excellent," Hyde said. "It shouldn't be long now."

Sam Baker cleared his throat to attract Hyde's attention.

"My money?"

"Oh," Hyde said, "yes, of course." He took a sheaf of

bills from his pocket and handed them over. "Make sure
you meet him, now."

"I will," Baker said, pocketing the money.

"Let me know where he's staying," Hyde said, "and
there'll be more in it for you."

"You got nothin' to worry about, Mr. Hyde," Sam
Baker said. "I'm right on it."

"I know you are, Baker," Hyde said. "I'm counting on
you."

As Baker walked away, Hyde was thinking that if he
didn't need the man to meet Adams at the station he
would have saved a lot of money by killing him and leaving him in the alley, just another victim of a random Barbary Coast murder.

TWENTY-SIX

At the last minute Clint decided to leave Eclipse in Denver, in the hands of the liveryman, Sykes, at the Denver House Hotel. Roper also promised to look in on the big black Arabian every so often, until he returned. Clint didn't want to have to worry about a horse while he was in San Francisco, and there were enough cabs in that huge city to make one unnecessary for travel.

When he got off the train in San Francisco with his rifle and saddlebags and stepped onto the platform a small man who looked something like a weasel approached him.

"Mr. Adams?"

"That's right."

"I'm Baker," the man said, "Sam Baker. Mr. Roper said I was to meet you and take you to your hotel."

"You're supposed to meet me and tell me where I can find Amanda Coates," Clint corrected. "I can find my own way to a hotel."

"Uh, yeah, sure," Baker said. "Can I, uh carry your saddlebags?"

"I'll carry my own," Clint said. "You got an address for me?"

"I do."

"Then let me have it."

The little man looked around.

"Right here?"

"Why not?"

"Well . . . we got a, uh, transaction to make, and I ain't exactly on good terms with the police around here."

"I see. How about my hotel?"

"Sure," Baker said, "let's go."

"No," Clint said, "I'll got to my hotel now and get settled, you come later ready to do business."

"Uh, when later?"

"After dinner," Clint said, "around eight."

"Okay," Baker said, "okay, I'll be there."

"Do you want to know the name of the hotel?"

"Uh, oh, yeah, sure."

"The Farrell House," Clint said. "Do you know it?"

"Sure," Sam Baker said. "It's a few blocks away from Portsmouth Square. It's owned by Duke Farrell."

"That's right."

"You, uh, friends with Farrell?'

"I am."

Baker nodded.

"That a problem?"

"No, no," the little man said, "no problem."

"Then I'll see you there."

"You, uh, want me to get you a cab and take you over there?"

"I can get around just fine by myself, Baker," Clint said. "I'll see you at the hotel later."

"Okay, fine," Baker said. "See you."

Clint left Sam Baker standing on the platform and went outside the station to get himself a cab. Baker was a paid informant of Roper's, not exactly a man who Roper trusted. He wasn't going to put any more faith in the man than he had to.

He got in a cab and gave the man the location of the Farrell House Hotel.

When Clint checked in he didn't know the desk clerk, so he asked for Farrell himself.

"Mr. Farrell is not here right now, sir."

"Is he out for the day," Clint asked, "or away for a while."

"He had to go out of town on business."

The clerk turned the register around so he could read Clint's name. When he did he obviously recognized it and his attitude changed.

"Mr. Adams!" he said. "I'm sorry, sir, I didn't know who you were. Mr. Farrell has left strict instructions on how you are to be treated whenever you come in, whether he's here or not."

"And your name is?"

"James, sir," the clerk said. "I just started here a few months ago."

"Can you tell me when Mr. Farrell will be back, James?" Clint could certainly have used Duke Farrell's help while he was in San Francisco.

"Probably in a few days, sir."

"All right," Clint said. "I'll take a room now."

"Very well." The clerk turned to grab a key.

"Is room seven available?"

The man looked at him over his shoulders and said, "Uh, yes, sir, room seven in empty."

"I'll take it, then."

"Yes, sir."

James turned and handed Clint the key.

"Do you need any help—" he started to ask.

"No," Clint said, "I've got it. Thanks."

"Uh, enjoy your stay, then, Mr. Adams," James said. "Anything we can do for you, just let me know."

"I will, James," Clint said. "Thank you."

Clint grabbed his saddlebags and rifle and went upstairs to his room. Not having Farrell to back him up might make things a little harder, depending on what happened in his first meeting with Amanda Coates. If he couldn't convince her to change her mind about him she might just send somebody after him right there in San Francisco, wanted poster or not. Sam Baker certainly would not be a reliable back-up.

He was tired, and decided to close his eyes for a little while before meeting Baker in the lobby. Who knew? It might be his last chance to close them for a while.

TWENTY-SEVEN

Clint went down to the hotel dining room for dinner at seven, and was finished and waiting in the lobby by eight, when Sam Baker entered. The little man walked in tentatively, as if he was afraid he might be seen.

"Relax," Clint said. "Farrell's out of town."

"Wha—how'd you know?"

"That you were afraid he'd see you? It's written all over your face. Why didn't you just tell me you didn't want to meet me here, if you and Duke have a history?"

"Ain't a history, exactly," Baker said. "I just ain't one of his favorite people, is all."

"Well, you don't have to be in order to help me," Clint said. "Just tell me what I need to know and you can be on your way."

"We, uh, got to exchange—"

"Oh, don't worry," Clint said. "I know I've got to pay you for the information. You'll get your money."

"Here's the address," Baker said, and handed over a slip of paper. Clint unfolded it, read it, then took out a folded bill and handed it to Baker, who tucked it away in a pocket without looking at it.

"Is there anything else I can do for you?" Baker asked.

"You can tell me who else you're working for."

"W-what?"

It was a shot in the dark, but if the guilty look on the man's face was any indication, it was a good one.

"You work for money, right?"

"Uh, yeah, b-but—"

"That means you'll work for anyone who pays you," Clint said.

"Well, I—"

"Don't deny it, Baker," Clint said. "Just think about it. If I find out you've been working both sides, I'll come looking for you."

"I, uh—"

Clint put his hand on the smaller man's shoulder, which made Baker flinch.

"Just think it over, will you?" Clint asked. "I'll be here for a few days."

"Um—"

He patted the shoulder and removed his hand.

"That's all. You can go."

Baker opened his mouth, but nothing came out. He stared at Clint for a moment, then turned and hurried out of the hotel lobby.

Clint didn't want to waste any time, but the address Baker had given him was a business one, and he wasn't going to find Amanda Coates in her office at this time of night, so seeing her would have to wait until the next day. That left him with an evening to kill. Normally, he'd kill it in the gambling establishments of nearby Portsmouth Square, but he couldn't risk that, not with those phony wanted posters still circulating. He'd be safer staying right in the Farrell House Hotel until morning.

Female companionship would have made staying in his room more palatable, but since he'd have to leave the hotel to find some it was out of the question. Unless . . .

He went to the hotel bar and entered with little hope of finding what he was looking for. The place was about three quarters full of customers, all of them men. There was no gambling in the Farrell House. That was supposed to be one of the benefits of staying there. It was close enough to Portsmouth Square so that people could find the gambling whenever they wanted to, but far enough away so that when they didn't want the gambling atmosphere they could get away from it.

He went to the bar and ordered a beer. He'd nurse it as long as he could and then go up to his room. He had a deck of cards in his saddlebags. Maybe he could entertain himself playing solitaire until he got tired enough to go to sleep.

The Farrell House had obviously undergone a change of staff since his last visit. The bartender was a young man he'd never seen before. Duke Farrell had once had a woman as a partner, but he had long since bought her out so that he'd be sole owner of the place. A beer and some solitaire seemed to be all Clint could hope for that night.

And he was going to have to be happy with that.

TWENTY-EIGHT

William Hyde gripped Amanda Coates by the hips and drove himself deep inside of her. The rounded cheeks of her buttocks slammed into his stomach again and again, filling the air with the sound of flesh slapping flesh. Amanda usually insisted on their sex taking place in this position, so that he wouldn't have to look at her ruined face while he was fucking her. Since he was servicing her he always went along with it. If he objected she might just find someone to replace him who wouldn't.

From behind she was as beautiful as ever. Her long, beautiful red hair was plastered by sweat to her gracefully arched back. Her buttocks were perfect orbs, smooth as marble as he ran his hands over her. He, however, considered her beautiful from any angle, but she would not be convinced of that.

He grunted as he drove himself into her, enjoying the way her slick insides seemed to grip him like a silken, gloved hand. He also enjoyed the grunting and moaning sounds she made. At one point she looked back at him over her right shoulder, so that he could see the smooth, undamaged right side of her face, and she was completely beautiful again. She was always very careful to keep the ruined side of her face facing away from him.

"Harder, damn it!" she snarled. "Come on! Harder!"

He obeyed her and grunted even louder as he pulled her to him with every thrust of his hips. Finally, when he could hold back no longer, he exploded inside of her and then slumped atop her as she lay down on her belly. He moved the damp hair off of her neck so he could kiss her there, but she jerked her head away and half whispered to him, "Get off me."

He took no offense at this. He could not afford to take offense at anything she said, for several reasons. First because she paid him, second because if he did she'd find someone else to see to her needs, and third and most importantly to him, because he loved her.

He slid off of her, careful to end up on her right side. She rolled onto her back, keeping the left side of her face away from him. She was breathing hard and it took a little while for her to get her breath back. He wondered what it would be like to have her on top of him, riding him up and down while he held her dangling breasts to his mouth so he could kiss and lick them, bite on her nipples. If only he could convince her . . .

"He's going to come and see me to tomorrow," she said, breaking into his thoughts.

"So you said."

"I want you there, nearby," she said, "but I don't want him to see you."

"All right."

"Can you trust your man not to give you away?"

"No," he said. "Not if Adams pays him enough. He'll give me up in a minute for enough money."

"Then get rid of him."

"I intend to," he said. "I only needed him today to meet Adams at the train station. I'll take care of him to-morrow."

"Good."

"What will you tell him tomorrow?" Hyde asked.

"The truth."

"Do you think that's wise?"

"Why not? He knows, anyway, by now."

"But to admit it . . . he might bring the law down on you."

She laughed and said, "Then I'll deny it, and it'll be his word against mine—and I'm an important figure in this city. Who do you think they'll believe?"

"You."

"Exactly. I can say anything I want when it's just him and me."

"Will you . . ." He stopped short of what he was going to ask.

"Will I what?"

"Never mind?"

They remained silent for a few moments, and then she asked, "Were you going to ask if I was going to let him see my face?"

He hesitated, then said, "Yes."

"Of course I am."

"Why?"

"He has to see what he did," she explained. "I want him to look at me and be horrified. That look that I hated to see in the eyes of men and women when they saw my face?"

"Yes."

"I *want* to see that look in his eyes," she said. "I *need* to see it."

They remained silent again for a little while and then he asked, "Can I stay tonight?"

"Yes," she said, turning away from him, "stay."

He slid up against her and spooned himself to her. The only time she allowed him to stay was when she wanted that, and he was only too glad to give it to her.

TWENTY-NINE

Clint didn't waste any time in the morning. He went to the address on Market Street right after breakfast. He found the office with AMANDA COATES on the door and entered.

"Can I help you?" a secretary asked.

"I'd like to see Mrs. Coates, please."

"Do you have an appointment?"

"No," Clint said, "but I think she'll see me."

"Your name?"

"Clint Adams."

"Oh, sir," she said, "you must have forgotten, but I do have you down here for an appointment this morning."

"You're right," Clint said, "I did forget. I've had a lot of things on my mind, lately."

She stood up and said, "Please follow me, Mr. Adams."

He followed her down a hall to another office with an unmarked door. She opened it and said, "You may go in."

"Thank you."

He entered and she closed the door behind him. He found himself in a small but smartly furnished office. There was someone sitting behind a desk, but they had their back to him, apparently looking out the window.

"Amanda?" he said.

The chair swiveled around dramatically and he was looking at her. She was a beautiful woman in her forties—beautiful except for the burned and ruined left side of her face.

"Take a good look," she said.

"I am."

Amanda was disappointed, because there was no look of surprise or revulsion on Clint's face.

On the other hand, her turn had been *so* dramatic that Clint felt she meant to shock him, so he kept his face as serene as he could. In truth, the reddened, shiny side of her face was, indeed, a shock, and he instantly felt sorry for her—and then he remembered that she was trying to have him killed.

"So," she said, "at last we meet."

"Yes."

"Have a seat."

There was one other chair in the room, situated right across from her. He walked to it and sat in it.

"What can I do for you, Mr. Adams?"

"You knew I was coming, Amanda—"

"Mrs. Coates," she said, cutting him off. "You don't have any right to call me by my first name."

"All right, Mrs. Coates," he said. "Have it your way, but you had me down for an appointment this morning. You were expecting me, so that means you know very well why I'm here, and what you can do for me."

She shifted in her seat a bit and he noticed that she was careful to keep the ruined side of her face toward him. He was sure that this was the opposite of what she usually tried to do.

"Ask," she said.

"You put out a phony wanted poster on me," he said, "put twenty-five hundred dollars on my head."

"Did I?"

"Yes, you did," he said. "I can't believe that after all
these years you can still somehow blame me for Ben's
death."

"It hasn't been so many years," she said. "Three."

"Okay, three," he said. "How can you possibly blame
me for what happened, Am—Mrs. Coates?"

"It's simple," she said. "He stood side-by-side with you
against four men in town, and then you just left. They
came back looking for you, and when they found out you
weren't there they settled for burning our home and leaving us for dead."

"What about those men, Mrs. Coates?" he asked.
"Don't you hold them responsible?"

"They'll be taken care of, eventually," she said, "don't
you worry about that. All the guilty parties will be taken
care of."

"But me first, huh?"

She stared at him for a few moments and he found
himself looking at her drooping left eye.

"Yes," she said, finally, "you first, Clint."

"Why do I get the feeling you didn't know Ben all that
well, Amanda?" he asked. She let the use of her first name
go, this time. "He didn't stand with me that day, he set
me up. I'm lucky I got out of there alive, and without
killing someone. Whatever he told you when he got home,
he didn't tell you the truth."

"He always told me the truth."

Clint laughed shortly then and said, "Wow, you really
didn't know him very well, did you? Ben Coates hardly
ever told the truth when a lie would do, Amanda."

"That was a Ben Coates you knew," she said. "Not the
one I knew."

"I was in that town ten minutes and he proved to me
that he was the same old Ben Coates," Clint said. "I came
there prepared to give him a chance, to meet you and see
his new life, but it wasn't to be. Even before I had gotten

there he'd managed to get himself in trouble, and he threw
me to the dogs in an attempt to get out of trouble. That's
the Ben Coates I knew, and I wasn't having anything
more to do with him."

Clint stood up and Amanda sat forward in her chair.

"The fact remains if you had been there those men
would not have taken their anger out on Ben."

"Those men were angry at Ben in the first place," Clint
said. "You better think this over, Amanda."

"I have thought it over," she said, "for three years."

"Your phony wanted poster is not going to work," he
said. "It's an obvious phony."

"To lawmen, maybe," she said, "not to regular men
with egos and money problems."

"You think that twenty-five hundred is going to do it,
huh?"

"Maybe I'll raise it," she said. "What do you think of
that?"

Clint looked around the office and said, "You seem to
have done pretty well for yourself, Amanda. Do you really
want to risk all of this on a vendetta over a man you seem
to have hardly known?"

She stood up and slammed her palms down on her desk,
leaned forward over them.

"Take a look at me, Adams," she said. "Take a hard
look. Do you really think this is just over a dead man?
Look at my face! You did this to me, and you're going
to pay for it."

"Amanda," he said, "you need help. I think a lot more
than your face was damaged in that fire . . . a lot more."

With that he turned and walked to the door. She was
screaming something at him as he went back down the
hall, but he couldn't make out a word.

When Clint Adams left Amanda's office another door
opened and William Hyde came walking in.

"Did you hear that bastard?" she shouted.

"I heard him."

"He has absolutely no remorse for what he did."

She was so angry she was not bothering to favor the left side of her face. Her chin was thrust out and she was shaking. He wanted to take her in his arms and hold her, soothe her, tell her to forget the whole thing. From the way he understood the story of her husband's death—and what he'd just heard Clint Adams say—he was sure that Ben Coates had gotten himself killed. He was also sure that the damage to Amanda's face was the fault of her husband—but he could never tell her that. For some reason she held the memory of her husband very dear, and anyone who spoke out against him was an enemy. William Hyde did not want to be Amanda Coates's enemy.

"I want that sonofabitch dead, William," she said.

"All right."

"I want him killed right here in San Francisco, where I'll be able to see the body and spit on his grave. Do you understand?"

"I understand, Amanda."

"Well then, go see to it!" she said. "I want it done soon."

"It may take a few days to set up," he said, "but it'll get done."

"It better."

He nodded, realizing that he had been dismissed, and left through the same door he had come.

Amanda walked to the window and looked down at the street. She waited until Clint Adams appeared and then pretended she had a rifle. She put one bullet into the back of his head with no problem. When he was gone she turned away and sat down at her desk.

William Hyde didn't think she knew the way he felt about her. He was in love with her, which she found amazing. After all, who could love what she had become? She was ugly, both inside and out. She knew this. There was no way to deny it, or change it, until Clint Adams was dead.

Maybe, after Adams was gone, she might give Hyde a chance, just to see if he could make her happy. Right now, however, there was no time for that kind of relationship. It was enough that he saw to her sexual needs, as well as her personal needs. There was no point in getting emotionally involved, just yet.

Her emotions were shut off—all but her hatred. That burned brightly within her, and only Clint Adams's death would extinguish it.

THIRTY

After Clint left Amanda Coates's office he found the nearest saloon, went inside and ordered both a beer and a whiskey. The intensity of her hatred had shaken him. It would have made her face ugly even without the burn marks. She was going to do everything in her power to see that he was killed. He knew this. He knew that he could not leave San Francisco with this matter unresolved. He could go to the police, but what would that accomplish? She was a prominent businesswoman in this city, and he was not even a citizen.

He would go to the police, though. He had to, just to let them know what was going on, because he knew there was no way he was going to leave San Francisco without killing someone. He couldn't kill Amanda herself, though, so how was he going to resolve this?

He drank the whiskey down in one gulp, then nursed the beer for a half an hour before leaving the saloon and heading back to the hotel. This was a tough one. In the past he'd had people intent on killing him, or on having him killed, but they had been men. He'd been able to handle those instances man to man.

He had no idea how he was going to handle Amanda Coates.

THIRTY-ONE

Instead of going back to his hotel Clint went to Police Headquarters to talk to someone about Amanda Coates. He ended up in the office of a Captain Nathan Beckett.

"We've seen the posters, of course," Beckett said, from behind his desk. "We had no idea who they had been manufactured by, but we knew they were phony."

"Amanda Coates," Clint said.

Beckett, a man in his forties with a receding hairline, scratched a spot on his head just in front of that hairline.

"Do you have any proof, Mr. Adams, that the posters were made and distributed by Mrs. Coates? I mean, after all, she is a prominent figure here in San Francisco, while you—"

"I understand your position, Captain," Clint said, standing up. "I only sought to keep you informed in case something happened while I was here. You see, I'm not looking for trouble. In fact, I'm looking to avoid trouble, but I'm not always able to do that."

"No, I don't suppose it's easy for you," Beckett said. "I appreciate you coming in, though."

"Sure," Clint said, feeling as if he hadn't accomplished

anything. He put his hand out and Captain Beckett stood and took it.

"Just one thing you should know, Mr. Adams," Beckett said, as he released Clint's hand.

"And what's that?"

"If you are, indeed, going to have some trouble with Mrs. Coates you might want to watch out for a man named William Hyde."

"Hyde?"

"That's right," Beckett said. "He's sort of her right-hand man, takes care of problems for her. If what you're telling me is true then you'd probably come under that heading for her."

"I would, indeed."

"Hyde is in his thirties, usually well dressed, dark-haired, very fit and competent looking. Did you see anyone like that when you went to see her?"

"No, I didn't."

"Well," Beckett said, "I'll guarantee you he was around, probably within earshot of your conversation."

Clint stroked his chin thoughtfully and said, "There was another door in the room. Could have led to another room."

"Probably did."

"Tell me, how do you know about this William Hyde?"

"Well, for a long time he was sort of a criminal."

"How is someone *sort* of a criminal?" Clint asked.

"He was involved in some shady dealings, but always seemed to walk the line, if you know what I mean."

"I think I do."

"A few years ago he suddenly appeared, working for Amanda Coates, who had appeared here with a lot of money and quickly established herself in the business community."

"Doing what?"

"Buying and selling."

"Buying and selling what?"

"Land, mostly," Beckett said. "Property with and without buildings on it."

"And do you know where her money came from?"

"No," Beckett said, "but then it wasn't my job to figure that out."

"I see."

"You might want to talk to someone who knows those kinds of things, though," Beckett said.

"Can you recommend someone with that kind of knowledge?"

"I have a friend who works for the *Chronicle*," Beckett said. "He knows these sorts of things because he follows the comings and goings in the financial world here in San Francisco. His name is Peter Beckett."

"Beckett?"

The policeman smiled and handed Clint a piece of paper with a name and address on it.

"He's my younger brother."

William Hyde was actually able to leave Amanda's office and catch up to Clint Adams on the street. If he hadn't been able to do that he would have established a tail on the Gunsmith later on, but as it was he was able to follow Clint to Police Headquarters. It made sense for Adams to go to the police, he thought, just to try to keep himself covered. Also, they'd be able to give him some information about Amanda. They might even warn him about William Hyde.

Hyde went across the street and got a table in a café there, one that afforded him a view of the front entrance to headquarters. If Adams had walked into the place and simply mentioned Amanda's name, then Hyde knew he was now talking with Captain Nathan Beckett. Hyde had crossed swords with Captain Beckett when the man was a lieutenant, before he began working for Amanda Coates.

Since that time Beckett had become a captain, and everything Hyde had done had an air of respectability.

It was Beckett's job, however, to look after the problems of San Francisco's elite, of which Amanda had become one. He might not immediately believe everything Clint Adams told him, but neither would he discount it out of hand.

Suddenly, with Beckett involved, killing Clint Adams would not be such a simple thing to arrange.

THIRTY-TWO

•

Clint presented himself at the offices of the *San Francisco Chronicle* and asked for Peter Beckett. He was given directions to the man's office. When he got there he found a man who slightly resembled the captain sitting behind a desk, every surface of which seemed to be covered with paper.

"Peter Beckett?"

Beckett looked up and said, "That's me. Who are you?"

"Your brother, Nathan, sent me over to talk to you."

"You one of Nate's men?"

"No," Clint said. "My name is Clint Adams. I'm—"

Beckett jumped to his feet and said, "The Gunsmith?"

"That's right—"

"Jesus," Beckett said, "sit down, sit down."

He hurried past Clint, closed the door to his office with a slam, then hurried back around his desk. He shuffled through the papers on the desk and eventually came out with some paper and a pencil.

"God, Nate didn't tell me he was settin' up an interview with the Gunsmith for me," he said, excitedly. "Let's start with you history—no, let's start with the first time you picked up a gun—no, wait—"

127

"I think you better wait, Mr. Beckett," Clint said. "I'm not here for an interview."

Beckett's face fell.

"You're not?" he asked. "Then why are you here?"

"I need some information. Your brother said you might be able to help me with it."

"Information? About what? Who?"

"Amanda Coates."

"Ah," Beckett said, sitting back in his chair, "the newest not so beautiful member of the beautiful people. Why do you need information on her?"

"She's trying to have me killed."

Beckett sat forward.

"There sounds like there might be a story in this for me," he said, "one that might get me off this desk and onto a new one."

"What kind of desk do you want?"

"That was just a figure of speech," Beckett said. "I need to stop writing about these society people. I want to cover the crime in the city."

"Well," Clint said, "what I'm talking about would certainly be a crime."

Beckett sat back again.

"How about an interview afterward?"

"Is that a condition of you giving me your help?"

Beckett scratched his head.

"Not exactly," he said. "I'll make you a deal."

"What kind of a deal?"

"I want the whole story of what's going on between you and Amanda Coates," Beckett said.

"And if there turns out to be no story?"

"Then you give me an interview."

"And that's the condition of your help?"

"That's it," Beckett said. "Take it or leave it."

Clint thought a moment, then said, "That actually sounds fair."

"Okay, then," Beckett said, folding his arms across his chest, "start talking . . ."

When Clint finished his story Beckett asked, "Are you hungry?"

"I could eat."

"Come on."

They left the building and led Clint to a small tavern not far from the *Chronicle* building.

"This where most of the employees eat?" Clint asked, as they entered.

"No," Beckett said, "this is where I eat. Most of the employees go the other way, usually frequent a couple of saloons. You can get a drink here, but the food is the reason I come."

Beckett walked directly to a table without waiting for someone to show the way. It was obvious he felt at home there.

"What are you drinking?" he asked Clint.

"Beer."

That was apparently what Beckett drank, for he simply had to hold up two fingers and a waiter appeared carrying two mugs of beer.

"The usual?" he asked Beckett.

"Beef stew," Beckett explained to Clint. "Best in the city."

"Sounds good."

"It is, I promise you."

The waiter left, promising quick service.

"Was there anyone else in the office when you spoke with Amanda Coates?" Beckett asked.

"No," Clint said, "but someone could have been listening."

Beckett nodded and said, "William Hyde probably was."

"Your brother mentioned him."

"He's Coates's right-hand man, and probably a lot more than that."

"Lover?"

"In the loosest sense of the word."

"What do you mean?"

"I mean, more likely than not, it's a physical thing, with no emotion involved—at least on her part."

"Do you know Hyde?"

"I know him."

"Friends?"

"No," Beckett said, "I don't mix with that crowd."

"I wouldn't think so, what with your brother being a policeman."

"Well, actually," Beckett said, "I don't mix much with that crowd, either."

"In any case," Clint said, "I'll appreciate anything you can tell me that might be helpful about Amanda Coates, or about Hyde."

Beckett spotted the waiter coming their way with a couple of steaming bowls and said, "Let me think about it while we eat, get my thoughts together, and I'll see what I can come up with."

"Deal," Clint said.

THIRTY-THREE

They followed the beef stew with some pie—peach for Clint, apple for Beckett—and coffee, and when the whole meal was finished Clint had to admit that everything had been delicious.

"However," he added, "this is not what I really came here for."

"No, you're right," Beckett said. "I'd have to do some research on Amanda Coates, Mr. Adams, but I know for sure that she came here with money."

"A lot?"

"Enough to buy her way into society, here," the newspaperman said. "Believe me, that would take a lot."

"She had a ranch with her husband," Clint said. "I don't see how that translates into that much money."

"Let me look into it and see what I can find out," Beckett said. "Maybe I'll come up with something helpful."

"And what about Hyde?"

"I can tell you about Hyde right now," Beckett said. "Coates has him trained, pure and simple. He was an animal before he met her. He'd kill you just as soon as look at you. She's got him wearing suits and using the right fork at dinner."

131

"Then the old Hyde would still be there, underneath the surface."

"Exactly," Beckett said, "and I think when she needs him, she lets him out. It seems to me she'd need the old Hyde to take care of you."

"And he'd be at her beck and call."

"Yes."

"But how did they meet?"

"That I can't tell you," he said. "It's a real beauty and the beast story, except which one's the beast?"

"I have to say," Clint said, slowly, "that I don't appreciate remarks like that about her injury, no matter what she's trying to do to me."

"Well, I can understand that," Beckett said, "but I wasn't referring to her looks. There's something wrong inside her, if what you're telling me is true."

"Up in your office you said something about an 'unbeautiful' member of the beautiful people."

Beckett lowered his eyes, having the sense to look sheepish at being caught.

"Guilty," he said. "I did make that remark, and I'm sorry. The fact is, she doesn't really socialize with that set, at all. She simply deals with them on a daily basis when it comes to business. This does not really endear her to the men or the women of that set. The men think she's invading their territory, and the women think that she is less than feminine."

"And how many of the women have actually seen her?"

"Not many," Beckett answered, "and when she does appear in public it's usually with a veil."

"She wasn't wearing a veil when I saw her."

"That's odd."

"Not when you consider that she was trying to shock me with her injury."

"And were you shocked?"

"Yes, but I think I hid it well."

"And did you feel any guilt?"

"No," Clint answered, immediately, "none."

"That's good," Beckett said. "If you did she'd be able to use that to her advantage."

"I think she was very disappointed that I wasn't remorseful," Clint said, and then, remembering her screaming as he left, he added, "*Extremely* angry."

"Well," Beckett said, "I've got to get back to the office. I've got work to do, but also all my research will be there. Shall we?"

'What about the bill?" Clint asked.

"They'll put it on my tab," Beckett said. "Don't worry about it."

They walked outside together and stopped on the street to shake hands.

"Where are you staying?" Beckett asked.

"The Farrell House."

"I would have pegged you as a Portsmouth Square man—unless you and Duke Farrell are friends?"

"We are. Is that a problem?"

"Not for me," Beckett said. "I expect you to have unusual friends. I'll get in touch with you as soon as I know something."

"I appreciate it."

"Meanwhile," Beckett said, "watch your back, or get someone to watch it for you."

It was good advice.

"I'll bear that in mind."

Beckett nodded, turned and started walking back toward the *Chronicle* building. Clint turned, looked up and down the street and then across the way. He'd had the feeling since leaving Amanda Coates's office that he was being followed. If he was, however, and it was by someone who knew what they were doing, *and* who lived here, the chances were slim that he'd spot them.

Finally, he turned and walked in the opposite direction.

From across the street Hyde watched with amusement as Clint Adams looked around. The man obviously knew he was being followed, but he'd never spot William Hyde, who was very good at everything he did.

Hyde let Clint go. He'd already seen him speak to both of the Beckett brothers. Starting tomorrow he'd have someone else tail the Gunsmith—someone almost as good as he was at it—while he came up with a plan for getting rid of him.

THIRTY-FOUR

When Clint returned to his hotel he was informed by the desk clerk that Duke Farrell had returned from his trip.

"When I told him you were here he asked me to tell him as soon as you came back, sir."

"Well, good. Tell him I'm back and I'll meet him in his office in half an hour."

"Very good, sir, I'll tell him. By the way, while you were gone a telegram came for you."

It was from Rick Hartman, the only person who knew where he was.

"Thanks."

Clint went to his room to relax for the half hour until he was to meet with Farrell. He was very glad that Duke had come back so soon. His friend might be able to add something to the mix.

From what he had heard from Beckett about William Hyde it would be easier to deal with the man than with Amanda Coates. At least he had experience with men like Hyde. But what would Amanda do if she sent Hyde after Clint, and Clint killed him? Who would she send next? Or would she quit?

No, he doubted she would quit as easily as that. He was

135

going to have to find out something that he could use
against her to make her quit, and that something was probably going to have to come from Peter Beckett.

He read the telegram from Rick, which told him some
of what he already knew. Rick had checked out Amanda
Coates and found out that she appeared in San Francisco
sometime last year with a lot of money and was now part
of the business world there. Rick said he would keep dig-
ging and let Clint know if he came up with anything else
helpful.

He dozed off sitting up in bed and awoke twenty
minutes later. He poured some water into a basin, washed
his face and went to see Duke Farrell.

"Clint!" Farrell yelled. He came around his desk and gave
Clint a bear hug. "I'm sorry I wasn't here when you arrived. I was actually looking at another hotel in Sacra-
mento."

"Are you planning to sell this one," Clint asked, "or
are you just expanding."

"Expanding," Farrell said, "or I was. Once I got a look
at the place I knew it wasn't for me. Come on, sit down.
How about a brandy?"

"Sure."

Farrell poured two snifters of brandy, handed one to
Clint and took the other behind his desk with him.

"Now what brings you to San Francisco within giving
me advance warning?" Farrell asked.

"It's kind of a long story," Clint said. "I'll try to give
you a short version . . ."

Farrell listened intently and did not interrupt once.

"Well," he said, when Clint signalled that he was done,
"of course I know of Amanda Coates, but I don't know
her personally."

"And Hyde?"

"Him I know," Farrell said. "He's a dangerous man, Clint, more so because you're on his home turf."

"I realize that. Also, you know a Sam Baker, don't you?"

"That weasel?" Farrell said. "What's he got to do with this?"

Clint told him that Talbot Roper had given him his name, and arranged for Baker to meet him at the train station.

"I would have thought Roper would have better taste in informants," Farrell said. "Don't trust him at all, Clint. He'll do anything for money, and he has absolutely no loyalties."

"That's what I figured when I met him," Clint said.

"Well, you figured right. Who else have you talked to?"

Clint told Farrell about Captain Nathan Beckett and his brother, Peter.

"I know both men. Neither will be dishonest with you, but you have to remember that Nathan is a policeman and Peter a newsman. That's where their loyalties lie."

"I realize that, too."

"So tell me, what are your plans?"

"Well, my next step was going to be to find someone who would back me up," Clint explained. "Someone whose loyalties I wouldn't have to question."

Farrell spread his arms and said, "You're in luck!"

"That's exactly what I thought when your clerk told me you were back," Clint said.

Farrell raised his glass and said, "You just tell me what you need and you've got it."

"Well, for one thing," Clint said, "I think I'm being followed, but I need to know for sure."

"We can take care of that tonight, or tomorrow."

"Tomorrow, I think."

"Tomorrow it is. What about the Square? Any plans to go over there?"

"No," Clint said, "not with those posters still circulating."

"I saw those posters," Farrell said. "Of course, I knew they were phony, but I had no idea how far reaching they were. I put out some feelers to see if I could find out where they came from, but I got nothing back. Roper must have really good contacts to have come up with Amanda Coates."

"He does."

"Well," Farrell said, "except for Sam Baker."

"Everybody slips once in a while," Clint said.

"Well," Farrell said, raising his glass again, "here's to no more slips."

"Amen."

THIRTY-FIVE

The next morning Clint met Duke Farrell in the hotel dining room for breakfast. They sat in the back, at Farrell's regular table.

"I've got a man you can trust," Farrell said over steak and eggs. "His name is John Shannon."

"Can I meet him?"

"No," Farrell said. "If you know what he looks like you'll be looking for him and you'll give him away. He's going to stay with you all day to see if you're being followed, and by who. He'll also be there to watch your back."

"Tell me about him."

"Used to be a Pinkerton, couldn't get along with Allan. Came here and set up shop for himself."

"I never heard of him," Clint said. Apparently the man had gone the same route as Talbot Roper, but had not made as big a name for himself.

"He hasn't been at it as long as Roper has," Farrell said. "Also, he doesn't want to become as big a name as Roper. He's a good man, I've used him before. I trust him, Clint."

"Well," Clint said, "if you trust him I guess that's good enough for me."

"What are your plans for the day?"

"I'm not sure," Clint said. "I can't make much of a move without information, and I'm waiting for Peter Beckett to come up with some."

"Why don't you just walk around and let Shannon do his job, then?" Farrell suggested.

"Walking around with those posters out there might not be such a good idea," Clint said.

"Don't go to the Square or to anywhere where you might be recognized. Stay away from Chinatown and the Barbary Coast. Those are the areas where somebody would most likely take a shot at you. Go down to Market, check in with Beckett, walk back real slow. By the time you get back Shannon should have your tail spotted. After that you can decide what you want to do."

"Sounds good to me."

"Don't worry, Clint," Farrell said. "Shannon will watch your back. You won't catch a bullet in the back unless it's from a rooftop, and nobody is going to be set up on a roof if they don't know you're coming."

"I'll still feel like I've got a target painted on my back," Clint said.

"Hell," Farrell said, "you feel like that all the time anyway."

"That's true."

They finished their breakfast and Farrell walked out to the lobby with Clint, all the way to the front door.

"Just take a turn around the city a bit, then come back," Farrell said again. "You'll be back safe and sound."

"See you later."

Clint went down the steps, turned to the left and started walking. In moments there was a man at Farrell's side. He was not tall, probably five-eight, in his thirties, and nondescript-looking which, in his chosen profession, helped.

"So that's the Gunsmith," he said.

"That's him."

"Good friend?"

"Real good friend," Farrell said. "I'd hate to lose him."

"Don't worry, Duke," Shannon said, slapping Farrell on the shoulder, "I've got his back."

"You won't, if you wait any longer to get going."

"Relax," Shannon said. "I don't want to be obvious. I've got to give his tail time to get going, too."

"Just make sure he comes back alive, John."

"I know my job, Duke," Shannon said. "Don't worry."

Shannon went down the steps, turned and went in the same direction Clint Adams had gone. Farrell stood at the door and watched until the man was out of sight, then turned and went back inside. He checked his watch, then tucked it back away in his vest pocket.

"Mr. Farrell?" the desk clerk called out.

"Yes."

"I've got some business to talk about, sir."

"Yeah," Farrell said, walking toward the desk, "okay, business . . ."

THIRTY-SIX

It was all Clint could do to keep from turning around and looking behind him over the course of the next few hours. It was a difficult thing to simply walk and walk with no definite destination in mind, never looking behind you even while you are certain you are being followed. He finally decided to take Duke Farrell's advice and go to the *Chronicle* building, even though he was certain Peter Beckett would have no information for him yet.

Beckett looked up from his desk in surprise as Clint entered his office, but smiled nevertheless.

"Twice in two days?" he asked. "To what do I owe the honor? You didn't think I'd have anything already, did you?"

"No," Clint said, walking to Beckett's window, "I just needed someplace to walk to."

"Why?"

"I'm trying to check on a tail."

"A tail—oh, you mean someone's following you?"

"Yes."

"I thought we determined that if someone did follow you it would be Hyde?" Beckett asked.

"Or someone he sent," Clint said. "I'm just trying to be sure."

"Well, that certainly can't hurt," Beckett said. He turned and looked over his shoulder. "So you only came up here to look out my window?"

Clint looked at Beckett and said, "I guess that's not very considerate, huh? I mean, this is where you work." He stepped away from the window. "Sorry."

"No, no," Beckett said, "my office is your office."

"Why so generous?"

"Because," Beckett said, sitting back and putting his hands behind his head, "I'm either going to get a story out of this, or an interview. I can't lose."

"As long as I stay alive."

"I hate to be callous," Beckett said, "but even that would be a story for me."

"You have a point," Clint said. "I don't suppose you've managed to come up with anything for me yet?"

"Nope, not yet," Beckett said. "It's a little soon."

"Right," Clint said. "Okay, thanks. I'll be talking to you."

"You can count on it."

Clint left the office, went downstairs and out of the building. Once again he made sure that he didn't check behind him as he walked away, leaving it to Farrell's man John Shannon to take care of his back.

That didn't make it itch any less, though.

This was the first day Jerry Delaney was following Clint Adams. He knew who Adams was, of course, so it suited him to follow the man and not get very close to him. William Hyde had not told him why he was following the Gunsmith, and Delaney didn't care. All he cared about was the money he was being paid. He was good at his job, because he was never curious about the people he was following.

After Adams went into the newspaper building he picked out a doorway across the street and settled in to wait.

John Shannon watched Clint Adams go into the *Chronicle* building, and watched the man who was following him take up a position in a doorway across the street. Shannon didn't recognize the man, but he appeared to be pretty good at his job. The one thing he did know was that it was not William Hyde, who Farrell had warned him to watch out for.

Shannon knew Hyde on sight, had crossed swords with him twice, once before he became attached to Amanda Coates, and once since. It was like talking to two different men. The lady had definitely had an effect on Hyde's attitude and behavior.

Shannon found himself a cozy doorway to settle into and waited for Clint Adams to reappear.

As Clint went walking down Market Street it was like a mini-parade behind him. Delaney came out of his doorway, crossed the street and started moving in Clint's wake. Behind him came John Shannon—not directly behind him though. Shannon chose to follow while remaining on the other side of the street. Much less chance of being spotted that way.

Clint considered hailing a cab, but that would have made it hard not only on the man following him, but on Shannon, as well. He decided to just stay on the streets and walk along a bit further. When it got to be a little later, and he thought that Shannon had enough time to spot the man following him, he'd grab a cab and head back to the Farrell House. There he'd have a meal and wait for Shannon to report in to Farrell. Maybe, at that point, he'd even get to meet the man. He was curious about a man who could impress Duke Farrell as much as Shannon did. Farrell knew Talbot Roper, and had worked with Able Tracker as well as Clint himself, so if John Shannon impressed him, this was a man he wanted to meet.

THIRTY-SEVEN

When Clint stepped out of his cab and paid the driver he took a quick look behind him. He didn't see any other cabs pulling up, so he figured he might have lost both his tail and John Shannon at the same time. He wondered if Shannon would have the initiative to keep following the man even though Clint was no longer in the picture. That way Clint could definitely put Hyde together with the man following him.

Then, as he walked to the door, he considered that maybe no one was following him today, at all, and this could have been a waste of John Shannon's time.

But no, he'd been able to *feel* someone behind him all day, and it hadn't been John Shannon. At least, he didn't think so.

Maybe these phony posters had made him paranoid, but whatever the outcome of the day's excursion there was no paranoia involved in Amanda Coates's attitude and intentions. The woman was definitely out to do him harm and he had to figure out a way of changing her mind before somebody else died.

Clint was going to check with the clerk to see where

Farrell was but the young man was a hair faster on the draw.

"Mr. Adams," he called out, as soon as Clint entered. "Mr. Farrell is in his office. He said to tell you to go right in when you got back."

"Okay, thanks."

Clint went past the front desk to the door to Duke Farrell's office, knocked and entered.

"Ah, back alive," Farrell said, graciously. "How nice."

"I took a cab," Clint said, "probably lost my trail and your man Shannon."

"I don't think so," Farrell said. "John?"

There was another door into the office from the back wall and it opened now to admit a man in his thirties, wearing a disarming smile.

"You're Shannon?" Clint asked.

"That's right."

Clint extended his hand and the younger man accepted it gratefully.

"How'd you get back here before me?"

"When you hopped the cab I assumed you'd be heading back here," Shannon said. "I got a faster cab, gave him a short cut, and here I am."

"So what's the story, John?" Farrell asked. "Is Clint being followed."

"Definitely," Shannon said, "and by somebody who knows what he's doing."

"Somebody you know?"

"No," Shannon said, "Hyde must have brought in some outside help. This guy is not in the loop, or I'd recognize him."

"He's definitely working for Hyde?" Clint asked.

Shannon looked puzzled.

"I didn't think that was up for debate," he said. "I thought we knew that Hyde was having you followed?"

"It's a virtual certainty," Clint said, "but it's not something I could take to the bank, if you know what I mean."

"Well, when you hopped that cab our man didn't show any initiative," Shannon said. "That's the one knock against him. He just sort of stood there and I decided to hop a cab myself and hightail it back here. Now, if you want to know for sure who he works for I'll have to follow him." He looked at Clint. "That means I won't be watching your back."

"Can you do this tomorrow?" Clint asked.

"Sure."

"Okay then," Clint said. "I'll leave here and find a place to hole up, where I can watch my own back. When he gets impatient maybe he'll head back to his boss for orders. That's when you can follow him and make sure we have this right. Hyde's working for Amanda Coates, and this man is working for Hyde."

"Then I can get back to you before you leave and we can head back here together," Shannon said. "I don't like the idea of you walking around this city with those posters out there."

"He's a man after my own heart, Duke," Clint said, then looked at Shannon and said, "My sentiments, exactly."

Duke Farrell smiled broadly and said, "I knew the two of you would get along famously."

Amanda Coates tossed her head back and reached for William Hyde's head. She was sitting on her desk with her legs spread and Hyde was crouched between them, performing oral sex on her in expert fashion. She didn't know where he had learned this, but often, when he was using his mouth and tongue on her, she lost sight of where she was. She didn't like doing that, but it was just too good to give up completely. Usually she had him do it either in her office, or in her bedroom, where it didn't matter if she drifted off, a bit.

She took hold of his hair and held his head tightly against her pussy, grinding her hips against his lips. The stubble of his face felt good on the soft flesh of her inner thighs. His tongue was stuck so far up inside her that she swore it was as long as his erect penis.

Speaking of which . . . he stood up at that moment and pushed her down flat on her back on her desk. Papers went flying to the floor but they paid them no heed. He positioned himself between her outstretched legs, pressed the spongy head of his huge penis against the moist lips of her pussy and entered her slowly. Inch by inch she took him into her steamy depths and then he was moving in and out of her, causing the desk to rock on its legs. It was, however, a sturdy piece of furniture and managed to stand up to the hectic pace they subjected it to. Before long he drove himself deep inside of her and stayed there, spurting his seed into her. She gasped and bit her lip, feeling as if her insides were being invaded by millions of tiny needles. Her belly trembled, her legs shook uncontrollably and it was all she could do to keep from screaming and bringing the whole office in on them.

"When does your man get back?" she asked, while they dressed.

"I guess that depends on when Adams goes back to his hotel."

"When are you going to do it, William?" she asked. "Or when are you going to have it done? Have you decided?"

"This is not something you can rush into, Amanda," he said. "First, I haven't decided whether or not I want to do it myself, so I certainly haven't decided when it will be done."

"But it will be done soon, won't it?"

"Yes, Amanda," he said, tucking his shirt in and looking around for his boots, "it will be done soon."

As he bent over to pick up his boots she grabbed him by the hair and turned his face up to face her. He could easily have broken the hold she had on him and put her on her knees in one swift move. He chose not to.

"If I ask you to do it yourself, for me," she asked, "would you?"

"You know I would, Amanda," he said. "You know I would do anything for you."

She released his head and said, "Because I pay you, right?"

He wondered, at that moment, what she would do if he told her he loved her, but instead he said, "Oh, yes, Amanda, because you pay me very well."

THIRTY-EIGHT

The next day went much the same way, only Clint did not walk to Peter Beckett's office. He went, instead, to Captain Nathan Beckett's office, at San Francisco Police Headquarters.

"To what do I owe this honor?" Beckett asked as Clint entered, immediately exhibiting a close resemblance to his brother, the newsman.

"Just thought I'd check in with you, Captain," Clint said. "You know, keep the lines of communication open?"

"Have you talked to my brother?" Beckett asked.

"He didn't tell you?"

"Oh," the policeman said, "I probably didn't mention this earlier, but my brother and I don't talk."

"Oh? Why not?"

"A falling out some years back," Beckett said. "Nothing to concern yourself with, Mr. Adams."

"Well, we have talked, and he didn't mention that little fact."

"And if you ask him about it, you'll get the same answer."

"Fine," Clint said, "I'll stay away from the question."

"Is he trying to help you?"

"Yes," Clint said, "but there's a price."

The captain looked away and said, "There always is, with him."

"Why did you send me to him, then?"

"Because he's a good man," Beckett said, looking at Clint again. "Good at what he does, which is picking up information. You needed help, and I thought he could help you, our differences aside."

"Maybe if you really did put your differences aside—"

Nathan Beckett held his hand up and Clint stopped.

"Sorry," Clint said, "none of my business."

"Right."

"Well then," Clint said, "I guess I'll leave you to your work."

"That's all?"

"Like I said," Clint replied, "just checking in."

"Well, don't fell compelled to check in every day."

"All right, Captain," Clint said. "I'll keep that in mind."

Clint turned and left the captain's office, but instead of turning left to go back the way he had come, he turned right, according to directions he had received from John Shannon.

"I know the inside of that building like the back of my hand," Shannon had told Clint at breakfast that morning. The meal had been Clint's idea, a way to get better acquainted with the man he was trusting his back to.

"And why's that?"

Shannon grinned and said, "I've been in and out of there under many different circumstances."

"Okay, so what do I do?"

"When you leave the captain's office there's another way out of the building," Shannon said. "Just try to make sure that no one sees you, because they don't like people to use it. It'll leave you on a side street and you'll be able to get away without being seen."

"And after that?"

"Come back here," Shannon said. "The rest will be up to me."

So Clint turned right instead of left, his eyes peeled for any policemen who might see him and stop him. Once he reached the proper stairwell, though, Shannon said he'd be home free.

"A lot of them use it as a way out of the building," he'd explained, "but no one uses it as a way in. There's very little chance that you'll run into anyone coming up while you're going down."

Clint was keeping that phrase in mind as he went down because if someone was coming up there was no place for him to go to avoid them. He'd have to bluff his way out.

Luckily, however, Shannon was right. He didn't run into anyone, and he made it safely out the side door and onto the side street next to the headquarters building.

He needed a few moments to get his bearings. He didn't want to come out on the wrong street and end up wasting the effort. Finally he picked his direction and came out on the street behind the building where—he hoped—no one was watching.

He looked both ways as he came out onto the larger street, then turned right and hurried along at a good pace without breaking into a run. He waited until he was several blocks from police headquarters before slowing to look for a cab.

He knew that sitting back at the hotel for the rest of the afternoon was going to be hard on him, but he needed to give John Shannon time to do his job. When a cab finally stopped for him he climbed in and gave the driver the address of the Farrell House Hotel. He sat back in his seat and wondered how long his tail would wait before he finally gave up.

THIRTY-NINE

Clint was more right than even he thought he'd be. Waiting at the hotel was torturous, so he went looking for Duke Farrell and found him in his office.

"How about some two-handed poker?" he asked.

"Clint," Farrell said, "I'm in my office, and I have a hotel to run."

"Does that mean no?"

"I've got cards right here," Farrell said, talking a new deck out of the top drawer of his desk. He cracked it and asked, "What stakes?"

When John Shannon entered Farrell's office a few hours later he found Clint and Duke playing poker on Farrell's desk.

"Got room for another hand?" Shannon asked.

"Sure," Clint said. "Have a seat."

Shannon pulled a chair over and Clint gave him a stack of chips.

"White ones are a hundred, blue ones are five hundred and red ones are a thousand," he said.

"Dollars?" Shannon asked.

"Of course dollars, man," Farrell said. "What do you think we are, a couple of pikers?"

Shannon looked at the chips, which seemed to be evenly distributed between Clint and Farrell and said, "Okay, then, dollars. Whose deal?"

"I'll deal," Clint said, "and you talk."

"I followed your man to a building on Market Street after he gave up waiting for you to come out of police headquarters."

"Amanda Coates's building," Clint said. He dealt out five cards for a hand of draw poker.

"Exactly," Farrell said, and then, "I open for a hundred."

Farrell and Clint both called.

"What did you see him do?"

"Well," Shannon said, "he went inside, so I went in after him. I saw him go to Amanda Coates's office."

"And what did you do?"

"I went in and talked to one of the secretaries there."

"And?"

"Our man's name is Jerry Delaney."

"How did you find that out?" Clint asked.

"I told you," Shannon said, "a secretary. Two cards for me."

"Three," Farrell said. "I told you this boy was good."

Clint drew one card and said, "So she just told you his name?"

"Well, she doesn't like him, and she doesn't like Hyde," Shannon said, "so I made like I was having trouble with them."

"And she didn't ask how come you didn't know their names if you were having trouble with them?" Clint asked.

"She was just real concerned about me and wanted to help," Shannon said. "Two hundred."

"Raise two," Farrell said.

"I raise two," Clint said.

"Call," Shannon said.

"Call," Farrell said.

"Ace high flush," Clint said.

"Beats three of a kind," Farrell said.

"Beats a straight, too," Farrell said.

"Your deal," Clint said to Shannon, raking in his chips. "So what happened after that?"

"Nothing," Shannon said. "Same game." He dealt the hand. "I left and came back here."

"That's it?" Clint asked.

"Open for a hundred," Farrell said.

"Oh, except that this secretary says she thinks that Hyde is having a, um, relationship with Amanda Coates."

"She's spreading rumors about her boss?" Clint asked. "I call."

"She sure is," Shannon said. "I call. Cards?"

"Two," Farrell said. "Isn't that what secretaries are supposed to do?"

"I don't know," Clint said, "I never had one. Three cards."

"Hmm," Shannon said, studying his cards.

"So what do you suggest as our next move?" Clint asked.

"Well," Shannon said, frowning at his hand, "now that we have Delaney's name let me see what I can find out about him. I'll take one card."

Shannon dealt them their cards and then took his own.

"Why don't you just sit around here tomorrow while I do some checking?" Shannon suggested. "After that maybe we can figure out a course of action to get you out of this mess."

"One more day inside?" Clint asked. "I don't know if I can do that."

"Duke?" Shannon asked.

"I bet two hundred."

"I raise three," Clint said.

"Hmm," Shannon said, again, "I'll call the raise."

"I call," Farrell said.

"Flush," Clint said. "Ace-King high." Those were the two cards he'd held.

"How does he do that?" Farrell demanded, throwing his three of a kind down on the table.

"I don't know," Farrell said. He also had three of a kind. "But can you answer me this?"

"What?" Farrell asked.

"These chips," he asked, as Clint raked them in, "aren't really worth all that money, are they?"

FORTY

It didn't take Hyde long to figure out what was going on after Delaney told him what had happened at the police station.

"Tell me exactly what happened yesterday, too," Hyde said, and listened patiently.

"All right," he said, when Delaney was finished, "you're done."

"What? Why?"

"You've been spotted."

"No I haven't," Delaney said. "Adams never saw me once."

"He didn't have to," Hyde said. "He's been leading you around while someone else spotted you."

"But how could—"

"Never mind," Hyde said. "Come with me and I'll pay you off, and then I want you to leave the city."

Delaney still didn't understand what was going on, but as long as he was being paid he didn't much care.

After Delaney left Hyde went out and talked to the secretaries who worked for Amanda Coates. As far as he could see Hyde was the only man who worked directly for Amanda. The only other men on her payroll worked directly for Hyde.

Hyde found one girl who had spoken to a strange man who had come into the office earlier in the day. It took some convincing but she finally admitted to telling him Delaney's name.

"Am I fired?" she asked Hyde.

"I don't have the authority to fire you," Hyde said, but he was going to talk to Amanda later about doing just that.

"All right," Amanda said, "I'll fire her before the end of the day. But tell me, can you figure out who was the man who talked to her?"

"I think so," Hyde said. "It sounds like John Shannon."

"Who is he?"

"A private detective here in San Francisco," Hyde said. "This makes sense, now. Shannon is friends with Duke Farrell, and Farrell is friends with Adams, who is staying at the Farrell House Hotel."

"Can we buy this Shannon?" Amanda asked.

"No," Hyde said, "I'll have to take care of him another way."

"This is taking too long, William," Amanda complained.

"Amanda," he said, "all I have to do is remove Shannon, and then Clint Adams will be next."

"Do you promise?" she asked.

He gave her a wolfish smile and said, "I promise."

FORTY-ONE

Clint spent the morning and afternoon of the next day trying to entertain himself while waiting for Shannon to return. He was finishing a late lunch with he saw Captain Nathan Beckett enter the dining room. The man looked around, spotted him and walked over to him.

"What can I do for you, Captain?' he asked. "Don't tell me you were worried today when I didn't check in?"

"I was looking for Duke Farrell," Beckett said, "but I guess you'll do."

"Do for what?"

"Do you know John Shannon?"

"I do."

"He's supposed to be doing some work for Farrell."

"And for me."

"Ah," Beckett said, "then you will do."

"Do for what?" Clint asked, again.

"Notification," Beckett said. "Shannon is in the hospital."

"What?" Clint stood up. "What happened?"

"He was shot."

"When?"

163

"Apparently this morning," Beckett said. "He was found lying in an alley this afternoon."

"How did it happen?"

"He was shot," Beckett said, "in the back."

Clint felt his face suffuse with blood, which drummed in his ears. His friend Wild Bill Hickok had been killed that way, shot in the back, but Hickok had not been shot while trying to help Clint.

"Damn it," Clint said, "I knew it."

"Knew what? That he'd be shot?"

"I knew that I should be taking care of this myself," Clint said. "He got shot trying to help me."

"That's a fair amount of guilt you're gonna be carrying around, then," Beckett said. "Maybe I can give you some good news."

"Like what?"

"He's going to make it."

Clint found Duke Farrell and the two of them accompanied the captain to the hospital. In fact, Beckett took them there in his buggy. Clint noticed that the two men exchanged very few words, and hardly looked at one another. There was a history there, but he'd ask Farrell about it later.

When they reached the hospital Nathan Beckett let them out but did not go with them.

"I've got work to do," Beckett said, "but I've got a man inside to keep me posted about what he says."

Clint and Farrell exchanged a glance, each feeling they knew who was responsible for shooting Shannon in the back.

"Don't you two get any ideas," Beckett said. "This is for the law to handle."

"Sure thing, Captain," Clint said.

The captain told his driver to move on and Clint and Farrell went up the walk to the entrance of the hospital.

"Hyde," Farrell said.

"I know," Clint said, "whether he pulled the trigger himself, or not."

"What are you going to do?"

"What I should have done in the first place, I guess," Clint said.

"And what's that?"

"Make Amanda Coates realize who she's dealing with," Clint said. "Make her and Hyde both know that I'm not going to stand for this."

"You mean," Farrell said, "you're going to live up to that reputation you've been hauling around for years, trying to ignore?"

Clint made a face and said, "I guess so. Let's go in and see how he is, though, before I decide to do anything."

The nature of the wound made it necessary for John Shannon to be on his stomach. His head was turned to the right and both Clint and Farrell could see that his eyes were closed as they entered his room. The policeman sitting outside the room had been alerted that they would be there, and they had no trouble getting in.

Shannon looked very pale. The doctor told Clint and Farrell that it was touch and go, as the bullet had been lodged in a very precarious spot close to the spine. He was going to live, but it still remained to be seen how much use of his arms and legs he would have.

"If I couldn't move my arms or legs," Clint said to Farrell quietly, "I don't know if I'd want to live."

"Maybe you feel that way, now," Farrell said. "Lots of people, when faced with the choice of death or any kind of existence, would prefer to live, no matter what."

They stood there looking at Shannon for a while, and then Clint said, "I've got to go."

"Where?"

"To see Amanda."

"I'll stay here until he comes to," Farrell said. He put his hand on Clint's arm. "Be careful. Watch out for Hyde."

"I think Mr. Hyde," Clint said, "had better start watching out for me."

FORTY-TWO

In the wake of the shooting of John Shannon, William Hyde decided to hire two men to remain in Amanda Coates's office, just in case Clint Adams decided to take the direct approach.

Which was, of course, exactly what he did.

Clint realized this as soon as he entered the office. It didn't matter to him, though, that he'd been predictable. He entered the offices and started for Amanda's private office. The two men left on guard by Hyde had been given Clint's description, but they hadn't been given very good advice. As soon as they saw where he was heading they went for their guns. Clint drew immediately and shot both men in the hip. As they went down he kicked their guns away from then, then continued down the hall to Amanda's office.

"What the hell—" she exclaimed as he burst into the room. "What happened out there?"

"You need two new guards."

"You killed them?"

"I incapacitated them," Clint said. "But they will need help getting to a doctor."

"What do you mean—"

Clint ignored her, went to the other door leading to or from the room and kicked it open. He found himself in another office, an empty one.

"Is that where Hyde was when we were talking?" he demanded.

"What if it was?"

"Look, Amanda," he said, leaning over her desk so that his face was only a few inches from hers. She shrank back in her chair, but never averted her eyes.

"You don't frighten me."

"I'm not trying to frighten you," Clint said. "I'm telling you I won't stand for this, anymore. Tell you boyfriend Hyde—"

"He's not my boyfriend."

"Boyfriend, lover, friend, employee," Clint said, "I don't care what he is. Tell him he's going to pay for what happened to John Shannon."

"You're going to pay for what happened to Ben."

"See, the difference here," Clint said, "is that Hyde has something to pay for, and I do not. I'm sorry about Ben, and I'm sorry about your face, but I had nothing to do with any of that. William Hyde, however, either shot or had someone shoot a friend of mine in the back. That's the act of a coward. If he wants me tell him he has to face me himself. If you want me dead, send him to do the job face-to-face. I'll be waiting at the Farrell House Hotel."

He straightened up, ejected the two spent shells from his gun, replaced them with live ones and holstered it.

"Why don't you just kill me?" she asked. "Nobody would bother you, then."

"Believe me, Amanda," Clint said, "I wish I was that kind of man, right now . . . but you know what? I'm not going to put you out of your misery. You're either going to have to do it yourself, or learn to live with it."

He turned and walked to the door, then turned back.

"I'll be waiting for him tomorrow," Clint said. "If he doesn't come I'll find him and finish this myself."

As he left Amanda stood up and began screaming after him.

"It'll never be finished until you're dead, Clint Adams. If you kill Hyde I'll just hire somebody else, and somebody else after that. This won't be finished until I'm dead, or you are!"

As Clint left the office he cursed the fact that he was too much of a gentleman to put a bullet in a woman's head.

When Hyde walked in he saw the blood on the floor, but the men had already been removed to the hospital. The secretaries had fled the office after the initial shooting.

"Amanda!" he shouted, running down the hall to her office. He found her sitting behind her desk, staring. "What happened?"

"He was here," she said. "He shot your men and then he tried to scare me."

"Did he touch you?"

"He didn't have to," she said. "My skin crawls whenever I think of him. You have to kill him, William."

"I'm working on—"

"No," she said, "no more delays. He said he'll wait for you tomorrow at his hotel, and if you don't go he'll come and find you. He wants you to face him because of what you did to his friend."

"Shannon," Hyde said.

"That's him. What did you do to him?"

"I put him in the hospital," Hyde said. "I got him out of the way."

She looked at him.

"He said you shot this Shannon in the back."

"Front, back, what's the difference?" Hyde said. "He's

out of the way, and Adams has nobody to watch his back."

"So you'll shoot him in the back, too?"

"If need be," Hyde said. "Facing him is playing his game, Amanda—"

"William," she said, standing up, "I don't care how you do it, just that you do it tomorrow! Or tonight, if you can."

"All right—"

"I want this to be over with," she said, "so I can get on with it."

"On with what?" he asked.

"Never mind," she said, dropping back into her chair as if she had simply lost all the strength in her legs. "Just go to his hotel and finish him."

"Were the police here?" he asked.

"They were here, but I told them nothing," she said. "Just that a madman broke in and shot those men. I don't want the police arresting him, I want you . . . to . . . kill . . . him!" Her voice rose with every word until the last was a shriek.

"All right, Amanda," he said. "Clint Adams will be dead tomorrow. I promise."

FORTY-THREE

Clint was at the bar in the Farrell House when Duke Farrell entered.

"How's Shannon?" he asked when the hotel owner joined him.

"He woke up, but didn't have much to say," Farrell said. "He was supposed to meet someone who might have some information about this fella Delaney, and even though he was alert he managed to get ambushed."

Farrell accepted a beer from the bartender.

"He didn't see who it was?"

"Didn't see or hear anything," Farrell said, and took a healthy swallow. "Hardly remembers getting shot. First he knew that he was, was when he woke up in the hospital. He's feeling real stupid and asked me to apologize to you."

"Him apologize to me? I'm the one who got him into this mess."

"Well," Farrell said, "if you want to get real technical about it, I'm the one who got him involved. You're the one who got me involved."

"Whatever," Clint said. "In the end I'm the one who's going to get us all uninvolved."

"How did it go at Amanda Coates's office?"

Briefly, Clint told Farrell what had happened, and about his conversation with her.

"So basically you went in there, guns blazing, and called Hyde out."

"I guess you could put it that way."

"Well," Farrell said, "that certainly was living up to your reputation."

"Only she wasn't scared at all, Duke," Clint said. "Not once. That's when I realized something."

"What?"

"She's only living to see me die," he said. "Once I'm dead, I don't think she'll go on much longer."

"Suicide?"

"I'd bet on it."

"Maybe," Farrell said, "once you're dead and she's faced with that she'll realize she wants to live."

"Well," Clint said, "I'm going to do my best to see that she doesn't get the chance to make that decision."

"You going to tell Captain Beckett about this?"

"Not a word."

"What about his brother?"

"I promised him a story," Clint said, "so I'll give him one—after it's all over."

"You got to be the one left standing to do that," Farrell reminded him.

"That's not something I'm likely to forget, Duke," Clint said. "Want to get something to eat?"

"I could use a bite."

They put their beer mugs down and went into the dining room.

FORTY-FOUR

Oddly enough Clint spent an easier evening, and then night, in his hotel room than the previous ones. He thought it was because he felt it was all going to come to an end the next day, but the more he thought about it the more he knew Amanda Coates was right. This would not end until one of them was dead. What good was it going to do him to kill Hyde when she would just hire someone to take his place? From everything he'd heard about Hyde the man appeared to care for Amanda. Clint went to sleep that night wondering how he could exploit that fact.

He woke the next morning feeling refreshed, and thinking that perhaps he had a plan that might work. He tried it out on Duke Farrell at breakfast. Farrell listened carefully, without comment, until Clint was finished.

"So, what do you think?" Clint asked.

"You really think that will work?"

"Why not?"

"Well, because not only are you not dealing with a normal woman, here, you're also not dealing with a normal man. Underneath the expensive suits of clothes

173

Amanda has William Hyde wearing, the man is still a thug."

"A thug who cares for a woman."

"This is a romantic notion you're looking to risk your life on, Clint," Farrell said. "I don't like it."

"I've got to try it," Clint said. "Anything is better than killing somebody."

"He shot Shannon in the back."

"I realize that," Clint said, "and I was angry about that yesterday."

"And not today?"

"Not enough to kill him, I guess," Clint said. "I think the problem itself is to blame for what happened to Shannon, and more people will get hurt—or die—if I don't solve the problem."

"And the problem is Amanda."

"Yes."

"Then the solution is easy."

"It is?"

Farrell nodded.

"Kill her."

"I'd have to kill Hyde, too, then," Clint said.

"So do it, and your problem is solved. I mean, look at this realistically, Clint. What's two more people if it will make the rest of your life easier?"

"One of them is a woman, Duke."

"Don't be such a damned gentleman all the time."

"You are."

"There's not some woman out there trying to kill me," Farrell said. "Believe me if there was I wouldn't be such a gentleman."

Clint sipped his coffee and considered what Farrell was saying.

"I tell you what," Farrell said, before he could speak again, "I'll do it for you."

"You'll what?"

"I'll kill her for you."

Before Clint could respond he saw Captain Nathan Beckett enter the dining room and look around.

"Hold that thought," he said, "we have company."

Beckett came over and sat down with them, uninvited.

"Coffee, Captain?" Clint asked.

"No, thanks."

Clint had still not seen the policeman and the hotel owner exchange a word, and he'd forgotten to ask Farrell about it.

"I checked in on your friend today," Beckett said.

"And?" Clint asked.

"He's got some movement of his fingers and toes," Beckett said. "The doctors are optimistic."

"That's great," Clint said.

"I thought you'd like to know."

"We do, of course," Clint said. "Thank you . . . but you didn't come here just to bring us some good news, did you?"

"No," Beckett said. "I came to see if this news would make any difference with you as far as going after William Hyde."

"What makes you think I'm going after William Hyde?" Clint asked.

"Because I know you're convinced he pulled the trigger, or had it done," Beckett said.

"Well," Clint said, "if that's the case what makes you think I wouldn't go after Amanda Coates? The orders would ultimately be coming from her, wouldn't they?"

"I don't think even you would kill a woman, Adams," Beckett said.

"Not even to save my own life?" Clint asked.

"Let's just say I'm trying to avoid both of us finding out the answer to that question," Beckett said. "Shannon did not see who shot him, so there's no way I can go after Hyde for this."

"I understand."

"I just don't want you going after him," Beckett said. "Do I make myself clear?"

"You do."

Beckett looked at Farrell and for a moment Clint thought they might actually speak to one another. Then the policeman stood abruptly, said, "Just remember what I said," to Clint, and left.

"Why is it you two never speak?" Clint asked Farrell.

Farrell looked at him and said, "Ask me some other time, when this is all over."

FORTY-FIVE

After Captain Beckett left, Clint rejected Duke Farrell's offer to kill Amanda Coates for him.

"It's a real friendly offer, Duke," he said, "but I don't think I'll take you up on it. Thanks, anyway."

Farrell shrugged and said, "The offer is still on the table."

"Well," Clint said, suddenly, "they come in twos."

"What?" Farrell asked.

"Pete Beckett just walked in," Clint said, and waved the newspaperman over. Beckett saw him and hurried over.

"Pete, do you know Duke Farrell?" Clint asked.

"We've met," Beckett said.

"How are you?" Farrell said. At least he was speaking to this Beckett brother.

"Have a seat," Clint said. "I was going to send you a message today. What brings you over here?"

"I have some information for you," Beckett said, "and I think you're going to like it."

"All right, let's have it."

"Your friend Ben Coates?" Beckett said. "Turns out he had a lot of money when he died."

"Where would Ben get a lot of money?"

"The word I got is that he inherited it," Beckett said.

"He had rich parents?"

"Wasn't from a parent," Beckett said, "it was from an old con man named . . . Streak something . . . Streak Evans."

Clint's eyes widened.

"I knew Streak," he said. "Where did he get a lot of money, and why would he leave it to Ben?"

"Those things I don't know," Beckett said. "This is the information I got—but this isn't the interesting part."

"What is?"

"It seems the law in Brown's Fork thinks that Amanda hired those three men to get rid of her husband."

"But she was disfigured in the fire," Clint said. "She wouldn't go that far to make it look real."

"Something may have gone wrong," Farrell said. "She does seem to genuinely hate you."

"I have a theory about that, too," Beckett said.

"What is it?" Clint asked.

"You kept her husband from getting killed in the saloon, right?"

"You could say that."

"Well, maybe the fire was never supposed to happen," Beckett said. "If you had not intervened maybe those three would have killed Ben Coates in the saloon that day. Either way, she inherited his money, came here with it and set herself up in business."

"If that's true," Clint said, "then her attitude is even more unbelievable—and she's sicker than I thought."

"So tell me," Beckett said, "why were you going to send for me?"

Clint saw a third man now enter the dining room, apparently looking for him. It was William Hyde.

"I think you're about to find out, Pete."

FORTY-SIX

Clint confronted Hyde right at the dining room entrance.

"Where do you want to do this?" he asked. It was obvious to him that the man was armed, but his gun was under his arm, and not on his hip.

"Is there somewhere we can talk?" Hyde asked.

"That's what you want to do?" Clint asked. "Talk?"

"Yes."

Clint turned and looked around. There were some empty tables in the dining room.

"Do you have any objection to talking right here?" Clint asked. He wanted to see if Hyde would balk at having Duke Farrell in the room.

"No," Hyde said, "none."

"Let's get another table, then."

Clint got the attention of his waiter and the man conveyed them to one of the empty tables. Clint was not able to see the entire room from there, but he could see Hyde, and Duke Farrell had his back. It would do for a short talk.

"What's on your mind?" Clint asked.

"I think we both want this to come to an end."

"We agree on that."

179

"First," Hyde said, "I had nothing to do with the shooting of John Shannon."

"We're not going to get anywhere if you start out with a lie," Clint said.

"It's the truth."

"I don't believe you."

"What can I say to make you believe me?"

"Nothing."

Hyde stared at Clint, who stared back.

"In any case," Hyde said, "I'm going to tell Amanda that this has to stop."

"Will she listen to you?"

"I think so."

"What do you want from me?"

"I want you to forget about her," Hyde said. "I'll take care of her."

Clint didn't believe a word Hyde was saying.

"All right," Clint said, "let's say I agree."

"Then I walk out of here. You'll never see me or Amanda again."

"That would be a comforting thought, if I could believe it."

Hyde rolled his eyes.

"There's nothing I can say to make you believe it, obviously," Hyde said, "so you'll just have to see it. I'll walk out of here and within a few days you'll see that I mean what I say."

"Fine," Clint said. "Walk out."

"You're going to let me go?"

"Yes."

"Even though you think I shot your friend?"

"Yes."

"Why?"

"Because I want this to end."

The two men stared at each other, and then Hyde stood up.

"I appreciate this," Hyde said. "I want to take Amanda away from here. I don't want her to end up dead."

"Neither do I."

Hyde hesitated, then said, "What would you say if I asked to shake your hand?"

"I'd say go to hell."

"You're a hard man."

"Remember that."

Hyde nodded, turned and walked out. Clint got up and walked to the other table to sit down with Farrell and Peter Beckett.

"What was that about?" Farrell asked.

"Lies."

"What lies?"

Clint told them what Hyde had said.

"And you don't believe him?" Beckett asked.

"Not a word."

"So what will you do now?" the newspaperman asked.

"Wait."

"How long?"

Clint looked at him and said, "It won't be long."

"He can't just walk in here and try to shoot you in front of a hotel full of people," Beckett said.

"That would be a story for you, wouldn't it? But no, you're right," Clint said. "He won't do that—but mark my words. We won't get through the night without something happening."

"In that case," Beckett said, looking at Farrell, "can I get a room in your hotel? I want to be around for the fireworks."

"Go out to the lobby and tell the clerk I said to give you a room," Farrell said. "I'll be out shortly."

"Thanks."

Beckett got up and walked out.

"What's going on?" Farrell asked.

"Hyde's trying a tactic that he's very bad at."

"Which is?"

"Diplomacy."

"And you don't think he means it?"

"Not a word."

"So what will you do?"

"Like I told Beckett," Clint replied. "I'm just going to wait."

FORTY-SEVEN

By midnight both Duke Farrell and Pete Beckett thought the day was over and nothing was going to happen. The three of them were sitting at a table in the Farrell House bar with mugs of beer that were less than half full.

"Maybe he was telling the truth," Pete Beckett said.

"No," Clint said.

"Why are you so sure?"

"Because it can't be that easy," Clint said. "It can't just . . . stop."

"Why not?"

"Because that's not how life works."

Beckett looked at Farrell.

"He's right."

"You're both pretty cynical."

"You're a newspaperman," Clint said. "You're not cynical?"

"Sorry," Beckett said, "that's my brother." He pushed his mug away. "I'm going to turn in. Let me know if anything happens."

"Just be ready to jump up at the sound of a shot," Clint said.

"Good night," Beckett said. "I'm going to think about my interview questions all night."

As Beckett walked away Farrell asked, "You agreed to an interview?"

"Only if he didn't get another kind of story."

"You felt pretty safe making that deal?"

"Yes."

Farrell yawned.

"I think I'll turn in, too. I know—I'll be up at the sound of a shot." He stood up. "Good night."

"Good night."

Farrell left and Clint sat alone for a few minutes, then took out his gun and checked the cylinders to make sure they were all loaded with fresh rounds. He was suddenly sure that whatever happened would happen in his room. He stood up and left the bar.

When he got to his room he stopped at the door and listened. Gun in one hand he used his key to unlock it as quietly as he could. He had left a lamp burning inside, and could see the light beneath the door. He watched for a few moments for shadows, but there were none. Abruptly, he turned the knob and darted into the room, dropping down to one knee, gun held out in front of him. The room was empty. He stood, closed the door and holstered the gun.

He went to the window and checked it. It was locked. He looked under the bed without feeling silly. He was about to check the closet when there was a knock at the door.

"Who is it?"

"Clint? It's Peter Beckett."

"What is it?"

"I have a message for you," Beckett said, "from my brother."

Clint walked to the door and drew his gun. He pulled the door open and dropped to the floor. The first shot went over his head. Hyde was standing behind Beckett, but Clint had a clear shot at one of his legs from between the newspaperman's. He shot the man in the knee. Hyde cried out and went down, releasing Beckett, who threw himself out of the way.

Clint stood and, as Hyde tried to bring his gun to bear, shot the man in the chest twice—once for himself, and once for John Shannon.

Beckett got to his feet in the hall and looked down at the dead man, then wiped sweat from his brow. Clint leaned over Hyde to make sure he was dead, then picked the man's fallen gun up and tossed it into the room.

Clint looked at him and said, "Was that message thing his idea?"

"Yeah."

"Good thing he didn't know that you and your brother don't speak."

"Good thing," Beckett said, as Duke Farrell came rushing down the hall wearing a dressing gown, "you did know."

The next morning Captain Nathan Beckett arrived to talk to Clint, who met with him in the lobby.

"The only reason your ass isn't in jail," Beckett said, "is that both my brother and Farrell back your story."

"I appreciate that. What about Amanda Coates?"

"She's gone," Beckett said. "Her office and her house are empty, nobody knows where she is."

"This isn't over for her."

"Maybe she just went into hiding," Beckett suggested.

"Until next time."

"And what will you do until then?"

"Well," Clint said, "I can't keep looking over my shoulder. Eventually those posters will stop circulating and disappear."

"One will turn up every once in a while," Beckett said. "Somebody will make a try for you."

"Somebody's always making a try," Clint said.

"So that's it? You're leaving?"

"That's it," Clint said. "I'll just have to be aware that I still have an enemy out there, one with money, and one with a grudge that she's built up in her own mind."

"I wouldn't want to be you," Beckett said.

"Well," Clint said, "the difference between you and me, Captain, is that you have a choice, and I don't."

Watch for

SAFETOWN

227th novel in the exciting GUNSMITH series
from Jove

Coming in November!

J. R. ROBERTS
THE
GUNSMITH